For

*La Santísima Virgen de
la Caridad del Cobre,
la Gloriosísima Diosa Ochún,
Mother of Cuba, of Love,
with Love,*

*and for
Mima,
who
basks in the
perpetual light of
this very Virgen, Cachita,
La Santa Madre de su devocion*

Otro Dia:

An Ode to the Queen of Cuba

By

Lorenzo Ramos

Lorenzo Ramos

Note: This book is best read
under the influence of
just a little too much
Cuban coffee.
Enjoy.
And Cuba libre.

Otro Dia

Beads of sweat flew from her body with every fitful shake of her head. Rocking her shoulders back and forth, she whipped her arms about like a ravaged bird, spinning the drummers into a frenzy with her shimmering feet. It was as though the drummers squeezed not their drums but the dancer between their legs, singing the rhythms into the night with exasperated, delirious smiles. They churned the *toque* into the air all the more intensely, keeping up with the melody and chime of her anklets. They were garlands, set upon the shining locks of her hair. Responses arose from the assembled, anguished cries of madness and devotion calling into the night—and it was only then, in the stories of their past come to life, that they remembered what was happening under the hot stars of Miami. It was not for men, not for women, but for those who brought us all here to begin with: the shining ones, the eternal music of the saints. This was theirs: young and beautiful, the *mulata* reeled back, shoulder by shoulder, looking back and forth with eyes that melted every heart in the room into sweet, sweet, awakening. Glowing in the honeyed flames of the music, the dancer was Mabel no longer but the Goddess *Ochún*, swollen lips and mischievous winks of gold flowing with thick, spiritual electricity into the sultry breeze.

"*Brrrrrrrrrrrrrrrrrrrrrrrrrrrrrah!*" She screamed. "*Awo, awo! Miel, denme miel! Dorada, enamorada! Awo, Awo, guemileré Changó!*" and she threw herself to her knees, shaking as if the earth itself were her lover, moving to the echoes of thunder. A dark man clad in red loincloths approached her, wielding axe and a bottle of liquor, stepping forward, stepping back, stepping forward, stepping back, and the drummers reeled on their instruments, tearing it apart into a mess of overtones until it pulled back once again into a completely new form, a chaotic *bembé* that made every spine in the room sizzle with fury into the sparkling night sky. Arms flew into the air.

"Ochún!" he said in a deep, strident voice. "You are the wife of Oggún, my brother, God of war and power. But tonight..." and his eyes narrowed into slits, "tonight you are my wife. Let him pine for his Mother Yemú in the darkness of his forge."

"It's all your fault, Babá," she answered shyly over the sway of the music, "was it not you who looked upon me while I was taking my bath?" Changó smiled, approaching the Goddess beat by beat, stepping forward, stepping back. Stepping forward, stepping back.

"*Changó!*" shouted one of the attendants. "*Alakata Lifubba! The King of Africa is in love!*" and the whole assembly began to jump forward and back, hunched over in primal sways that moved the drummers higher still. The man bit down on a thick, leafy cigar and spewed sparks and spittle with bold, strident steps, spurting *aguardiente* out of his mouth into the night sky and all over the shining black body of Ochún. He plunged his hands into a bowl of honey at her feet, rubbing it all over her as she swayed below him back and forth. She beckoning him come down to her, with sticky pulls of his delighted hands up her hips, over her neck, across the swell of her breasts. Honey bubbled from beneath his fingertips as he pulled her up to his chest, and together they began to move in rhythm, smacking as they swayed about in unison, again and again. How wanton this dance between the Queen and Her lover! The heat of an affair so divine, even the Gods could not bear to turn their gaze aside.

The back of people's necks began to churn with energies unfathomable, and sporadically, the assembled began to sway and scream demands from the beyond, the *Mas Allá*. Ancestors, spirits, were mounting, *timbelese Oloddumare*. Men gnashed at the cigars they had been smoking, and others grabbed the heads of the poor drummers, yelling at them to play their songs. Others had begun to chant Lukumí hymns in time with the chants, praying and whooping for their needs, for purity, victory, triumph and prosperity. It was this story remembered by the initiates tonight, that the beauty of Changó and Ochún's torrid affair was nothing short of *chaos*, sheer passion that cast all laws and obligations aside in the name of raw power, *Aché*, and that this, veiled upon the face of wisdom, was the stuff of life. *Sweet it was to live in sin, for these were the essence of all virtues*, a mirror of the universe in the black of your eye. The spirits had come to dance for they knew, to celebrate the stories told for thousands of years, to remember the stories of the first ones, the ones that shine.

Amidst screams and spurts of alcohol, Ochún began wailing something over and over again in the midst of her dance. Changó turned a bewildered smile towards her, for this was nothing from the myths. This was nothing from the ceremony. It was something strange, unbridled, unprecedented, something that made even the King of Africa listen closely to what it was. He commanded her gaze and she looked up into his eyes, her eyes troubled, shining.

"*Banle mi, banle mi Babá,*" she sang, over and over again. *No lo sé.* I do not know.

"What is it, Ma?" a woman beckoned from the crowd. "What plagues the mother of the universe, She who has made all questions and their answers as well?"

"*Banle mi, banle mi!*" she crooned in response, and with that she threw herself from her lover, dancing alone in steps that stopped the entire crowd from the antics their spirits were imposing on them. "*Brrrrrrrah! A-sssssssssssssA!*" They watched, transfixed, as she jumped over and over again into the air, spinning about and arching her chest back and up into the sky, tearing her clothes apart with her slender fingers, her white teeth, and sparkling honey glistened into the bewildered eyes of the assembled, smeared across the fertile womb of the Goddess, holder of all secrets.

"They speak to me, they speak to me and I have come to tell!"

The light left her eyes as she fell to the ground, where all but the *ileké* around her neck became smeared with dirt from the ground. "Mayi," the woman asked again, "what did you hear? What pulled Yeyé from our dance tonight?"

"Al que no aprende vivir aqui, le dan una oportunidad en la muerte." One who fails to learn how to live is given an opportunity in death. She snapped her head back, breathing in with a long, rich hiss. "Ofelia stayed in tonight, they speak to her and they will speak to her in dreams."

"Ofelia? The priestess of Yansa?" asked one of the drummers.

"*Si*, Ofelia. We can not borrow intelligence but *she* will give it, *your* contempt is his gift, and *he* has been given license by Olofin to give and take as he *pleases*." A woman handed her a glass of water, which she sipped softly before continuing. She looked up, and smiled into the sky. "Elegguá, *he* has started to play." The priests touched their heads at the mention of His name, muttering calls of *'Eshubara!'* and *'Laaaa-roye!'*

"We must finish," the priests then said, almost in unison. In the higher aethers spirits swirled about the crowd like lovers separated too soon from the mystical union. Lights flickered, and tobacco sparked furiously at the end of thick lips.

"*No*," said the woman who had danced Ochún. "They have spoken, and I..." She finished her drink. "I hear ugly things. The sun rises over every night, but for some the night is long, and dark. We are finished for tonight. None shall divine until the sun rises again." There was a stillness amongst the assembled, and the woman Mabel looked around, but into no one's eyes. "Make the rest of the offerings, but the dance is done under our feet. Babalu, too, shall arrive at *his* pace." And the hot stars glistened in the night, for they knew that this dance of life was but the play of children, and that the mischievous one, little Elegguá, had turned his smile upon the colorful sorrows of Southwest Miami.

A thousand rattles hiss!
Coconuts fall to the ground, ripe,
Holding the balsam of all tranquility.
Elegguá, it is your name we sing.

The stars passed over, and night turned to day once again as it would always do. People rose from their beds, brushing their teeth, saying prayers to their Gods and sending hot plumes of espresso and tobacco smoke into the air. An old man sat on the floor, bare feet splayed out before him, calloused with the wisdom of the four directions. Between his legs sat a round tablet, a board of darkwood carved with signs of his past, stories too old for words. He fished a handful of *kwele* from his yellowed pouch, touched them to each of the four sides of the tablet muttering prayers, and tapping them to his temples, his brow, his shoulders, his heart, he kissed them and let them fall to the surface of the wooden board. He smiled, and threw them again. Smiled even more.

"*Ifá...*" he laughed to himself, "you know better than to get between a woman and her man. Good morning to you, your will is my volition," and his eyes squinted with the laughter of the past. The sun sparkled through dark windows.

~*~

The smell of stale cigarette smoke hung in the room like a subtle presence, a musty, ashen spirit that lingered in the corner and curled around the blades of a fan that hadn't worked for years. An ashtray sat on the darkwood coffee table topped with a thick pane of glass, green at the edges, filled with the charred remains of some horrible accident, smudges of resin and ash painting hideous forms along the sides of the little dish. It reminded Silvia of the cremation grounds she had seen on TV, little cigarette butt bones sticking out of the remains of people's bodies. She wouldn't smoke another one. Set her pack next to the ashtray. Silvia had only been in two places her whole life: Cienfuegos, Cuba, where she was born and raised, where she had met her husband Orestes, 'Chiche' to the family...and Miami, Florida, where they had lived in the same house since the ninety miles of the Mariel some twenty or thirty years ago. They had come to the United States in hope of realizing the promises of American life, fantastic dreams of greener grass that communism had taken away from them one law at a time. On this side of the ninety miles, however, things were just as difficult, but in a different way. Silvia had started smoking openly just after a few months of living in the USA, forsaking years of hidden revelry with her cousins after her parents went to sleep. It got worse after she got married, though, for she realized that she would always smoke at the times when she thought she was supposed to be making love to her husband, late at night, staring into the black expanse of stars and dust. Only here, in Miami, did the ashtray begin to hold the charred remains of a horrible accident. It was here, in Miami, that Silvia saw Chiche faced with a world that was not his. It was here that the Cuban ways of old, of 'sitting back and letting me take care of it' turned into a prison whose guard was its very prisoner, and Chiche would bring food for the both of them as best he could. It was here, that away from their families, there was no one to turn to, and to no one did they turn for years, until more of them crossed the ninety miles. And it was here, within the four walls of Silvia's cloudy crystal ashtray, that she was somehow responsible for it all. It crushed her soul, little by little, day by day, and though she thought it was the cigarettes, to the spirits who had begun to observe her every action it was much, much more.

Creelo o no, la verdad sigue igual.
Believe it or not, the truth remains the same.
La vida es para aprender, para amar.
Life is for learning, for loving.
Y el maestro tiene dos caras, miralo con cuidado.
The teacher has two faces, behold them with caution.
Duerme con un ojo abierto, como él, y permanescarás despierto.
Sleep with one eye open, like him, and you shall always be awake.

In truth, Silvia resented the fact that they had come to
America, but she dared not tell Chiche for it would start him on
another rant about how horrible Cuba was, the hunger, the
craftiness the people had been driven to, the squalor, the condom
pizzas and the blanket sandwiches, and frankly, she'd had enough
of all of it. She knew the stories. Too well. And Chiche, she knew
Chiche too well. Too well. The old Cubans say that a mother
knows her children better than they do themselves, and though
Silvia knew hers to their very vicissitudes, it was Chiche who she
knew best. In many ways he was just another child she was
raising, a child with a balding head and old, drooping balls, who
brought bread home selling vacuum cleaners to people around
Miami-Dade county and still couldn't manage to dress himself
like a man. A child who had dominion over her, a child who kept
her prisoner in the house with her duties, I shall strive and vow to
protect you from the dangers out there, this confusing world of
America. She was a slave, the central pillar of the household, and
no one asks pillars how they're doing...they're just pillars, made
for one thing and very well can they do it! In fact, they're
expected to do that and little else. She hated this not about
herself, but about Chiche, for it betrayed his impotence of
character, and she would always tell him in the mornings, when
he would wake her up with complaints that she hadn't laid out
his clothes for the day:

"*Hijueputa,* your clothes are right there! I am not your
Mami, cojones! Treat me like you did when you married me for

13

once, ah? I didn't climb on top of myself that night..." and she would throw her head back on the pillow, in defiance. No breakfast for you, *títere*.

Chiche would laugh and poke her on the nose every time, a little gesture of affection that drove Silvia up the wall—"Do I look like a Goddamn lottery machine?!" —and she would glare at him with the look that everyone knew could kill birds. They said this because one hot summer morning a long time ago their old parrot Timbita was squawking loudly for hours at a time as she liked to do, and after hours of yelling back, Silvia jolted herself around with the full force of her soul and shot her a gaze that teemed with the profundities of her innermost hatred—and the bird died. The story became famous around the community, told at holidays over and over again every year to drunken laughter, but everyone knew how terrible it was, this look of Silvia's, only years of austere bottling-in of anger, frustration, contempt and resentment could harbor such a ray, not to be confused with the evil eye, and in honor of its first victim they aptly named it '*La Timbita*'.

"*Negra,* you've always been my *Mami. Dale,* serve my breakfast, I've gotta go."

Silvia smoked another cigarette, twirling the lighter between her fingers as she sat quietly. It had her sun-sign on it, Capricorn, and she put it down on the darkwood coffee table with a clink that seemed too loud for the physics involved. It was her favorite thing about the table. She drew deeply on the cigarette, feeling the familiar sting in the middle of her chest, that lovely feeling that hurt in a good way, I'm still here, that feeling that told her she took in just a little too much smoke. It was her way of crossing the line, rebelling against life, against death, and sometimes it made her lips tingle for minutes at a time. In the house all day, it was all she could do to cross the line. She smoked

herself into pain and embraced it with all she had within herself—
smoke—looking idly into the spackled ceiling to the sound of TV
commercials. She exhaled the flurry of smoke into the still air of
the morning and pressed her lips to the flimsy paper filter once
again, drinking the smoke like a child would drink milk.

"*Ay, pinga,*" she sighed into the ceiling, sending a
mushroom of smoke halfway there. Silvia was alive, and she
listened to kids banter on the toothpaste commercial behind
closed eyes as she hovered to the soft beating of her heart in her
self-created void, the closest thing to peace she knew. It was only
here that she could allow herself to feel serene, a body entombed.
Her lips, they tingled, and her legs were vibrantly soft, relaxed
and spread, enjoying the air that drifted between them. No one
else is here to see...she opened her eyes, and right at that moment
the ash broke off the end of the cigarette and fell into her lap with
a little pat she heard but didn't think she should have. She
brushed her *bata* off with a calloused hand, pulling the cigarette
from her lips. They stuck to the filter until she grinned them off,
setting the smoke into her little cremation ground, tapping the
glass-top coffee table a few times with her lighter to hear the
sound. It was time to make lunch—Chiche would be home soon.

It had been a long time since Silvia actually ate lunch.
Back in Cuba she used to cook three meals a day for the family
and partake happily, but now that the kids had grown up it was
only for her and Chiche, and she didn't care about eating that
much, at least not meals. It was Chiche who needed to eat and get
back to his sales, and his lunch was the same every day—
breakfast again with last night's leftovers. You see, Chiche was a
firm proponent of the fact that lunch was between breakfast and
dinner, and he enjoyed it so everyday. Last night's *congrí*, but not
the meat—maybe a piece of *yuca* or a couple of refried *mariquitas*,
which made them crispier—and another mug of *café con leche* with
a big piece of Cuban bread. Every morning Chiche went to the

bakery nearby, *La Rosa,* to pick up Cuban crackers, a loaf of bread and sometimes, if the *ambiente* was favorable, some coconut or guava *pastelitos* – he hated the guava and cheese ones, the *refugiados.* "They remind me of politics." *Refugiados,* refugees. "I'm not a *fockeen* pastry." Silvia always ate most of the crackers, and Chiche would eat a third of the loaf in the morning, a third at lunch, and the last piece for breakfast the next day, whereupon he would bring the fresh loaf at lunch time and carry the cycle on in this fashion. It was a fresh loaf at lunch day, and Silvia muttered quietly to *La Virgen* that he should bring some *pastelitos* because nothing would make her day like a fresh guava pastry – '*Ay Virgensita, esos pastelitos de guayaba'* – and she fantasized about it as last night's *congrí* sizzled in the pan, crackling and popping and burning her resinous nostrils until Chiche came through the door and she turned the fire off. He held in his hands a loaf of *pan Cubano*...and nothing else. Silvia looked to him and back to the sputtering pan and let out her monosyllabic, if that, greeting, acknowledgement, scoff. It was everything, everything good, everything bad, anything the other wanted it to be, rebellion, surrender, apathy...that was it, simply:

"*Hmph.*" *No Pastelitos.*

Chiche put the loaf down on the sofa by the darkwood coffee table and took his dark blue work jacket off, the one with a happy vacuum cleaner on the front pocket, *Huracán, el viento que te limpia,* setting it down with a groan of exhaustion.

Hurricane Vacuums, the wind that cleans for you.

"You didn't bring any *pastelitos.* Or *galletas.*"
"*Psssh,*" whistled Chiche, "*no seas mensa.*" Don't be stupid.
"*Pero el pan si,*" Silvia said, more to herself than to Chiche.
"Of course, *Negra,* what's wrong with you, is my lunch ready?"

Silvia's tongue burrowed into her cheek, her teeth aching to bite down as hard as they could.

"Eh?" Chiche untucked his shirt. *"Oye, que me tengo que ir!"* I've gotta go...

"Pues sientese ahi y comete un cable, viejo de mierda!"

"Ey, I'm just hungry..." and he smacked his lips — *tss* — "been working all morning, and this *Negra* complains about making me lunch, you know, *que barbaridad, oistes, mi viejo —"*

"Callate, niño, carajo!" said Silvia from the stove. Shut up, child..."You just go try and sell people vacuum cleaners. So their wives can just sit there and keep the house clean, and make them lunch, and breakfast, and raise the kids, and do everything for the house and all they want is a Goddamn *pastelito* every now and then, and you don't have that, no, you just have vacuum cleaners. Chores. Rrrrrre*pinga*." She poured the steaming *congrí* onto an old plate with faded little flowers on it and took the *café con leche* out of the microwave where it was keeping warm. *"Dale,* your lunch is ready."

"All I want is a plate of food and I gotta hear Castro talk about the *pueblo* and the past, *coño'e su madre..."* He sat into his green corduroy chair where he pulled his shoes off and plopped his feet onto the matching footstool that sat ever faithfully before it. Just like always. The fan hovered above them quietly, listening to everything with the satisfaction of a little child.

"It's good to be home — *aaaaaay..."* and he closed his eyes, wiggling his toes inside of the pale brown dress-socks he had worn for five days now, just like always. He wore only dress-socks because they were smooth and sleek on his feet. And they took longer to start smelling bad, or more, for others to notice. The first questionable sniff he got from anyone, he knew it was time to wear a new pair. The socks, though, were one of the simple pleasures he entertained that kept him smiling. It was like a little secret that Chiche got to keep from all of his customers and all of the fat women at the bakery and the guy with the hairy ears at Solano's. His feet always felt good inside of his shoes, and none of them knew it. It was like wearing silk underwear, he imagined, but for the feet.

"*Hmph*," he growled, clearing his throat. "*Negra...*" and there was an unbearable, illogical silence. "*Negra...*"

"*Que?!*" Silvia screamed, unable to bear it any longer.

"*Dale.*" *Su pinga!* Chiche listened to Silvia set the table up behind closed eyes, plates and silverware upon greasy doilies that were forever on the breakfast table, more than the wood itself. He knew precisely when she was done from the sounds, and he opened his eyes when he knew she would be right in front of him on the way back to the stove to clean up the pans and the *cafetera*. He grinned when she looked at him peeking through one eye. She did not. *Ay mijito*...just like always.

Chiche ate his lunch in the unconscious ambience of TV commercials, looking through the glass door to the backyard and up at the old pictures of Cuba, sipping his *café con leche* between bites. The sky shone brightly outside, but inside it was dark and shady, cool for comfort, a solitary burrow. Silvia took the plates from the table, greasy residue reflecting the light outside as she carried them to the sink. The backyard was small, and the grass had never been tended to, not since they moved into the house some twenty or thirty years ago. Weeds flourished amidst the defeated grass, and patches of yellow-brown showed where the neighbor's dog had pissed in the past six months. It liked to crawl through the collapsed picket in the fence, hitting the same spots over and over again. Some of the patches were reduced to cakey dirt by now, cracked and baked in the summer sun like Indian bricks forgotten long ago. Neither Chiche or the neighbor had gotten to fixing the collapsed picket, though they talked about it quite often when passing each other in the yard. An old birdcage

Chiche built years before sat by the fence in a corner, a wooden box with chicken wire along the long sides of the massive rectangular structure that no longer housed any birds. He used to have canaries, but they died off slowly, mauled in the night by the neighbor's cat, all except for the last one, who died one Christmas Eve in the bitter cold of the night. They didn't find the little yellow puff until the morning, when they realized with tears in their eyes that cold could kill people. Or birds. You see, in Cuba it was the heat you worried about. Chiche simply crumpled it in a rag and stuffed it into the bottom of the garbage. Silvia remembered him cursing when he sneezed on the way to the bathroom and threw his hands up into his face out of instinct. She laughed to herself from the sink, and had one not known what was going through her head at the moment, she would have seemed like she was enjoying her chores.

He choked on the bite of food he had tried to swallow, fighting through the discomfort silently. Silvia watched him from the sink, averting her gaze when he looked up and spoke, clearing his throat. "*Oye, rrhrrrm, Negra, ah-hrrrrm!* Your *congrí* is better the next day than it is fresh, *rrrHRRM!*" he smiled with watering eyes, and he sat back into his corduroy chair, picking his teeth with his fork. The shiny tablecloth was full of creases, littered with crumbs from the *Pan Cubano* and Silvia's crackers from an hour ago.

"*Mmhmm.* Your daughter, *Yennifer,*" for that was how Silvia pronounced it, *YEN-i-ferrrrr*, "said she was going to be home early today. Maybe we'll eat dinner together..." Chiche flicked his eyebrows into the glass door, not saying a word. Silvia washed the dishes in the musty silver sink. The tap never ran hard, only soft and steady, a little cloudy, sometimes warm, sometimes cold, making even the dishes a chore that depended on something else. She turned it off as she soaped the wash and scrubbed the residue off the flowery plates.

"Has Tico called today?" said Chiche, hiccuping with a

stir. He sneezed.

"No, he said he'd be at the *café*…he'll call later," answered Silvia as she dried the plates and put them back into the cupboard next to the stack of bowls. She smiled. "Maybe he'll come eat, too."

"Writing, at the café…he's so full of shit, with his religious crap. But *you knooooooooooow?!*…he gets by, the other nuts read his garbage…*pisses me off.*" Chiche hacked into a napkin, checking it out before he crumpled it into his fist, staring out into the backyard. "Pisses me off."

Tico, Silvia's oldest, whose baptized name was Alberto, was a hopeless *romantico* who had an oceanfront condo he shared with his lover Angelica. A success story, God-bless *el Yoo-Es-Ey!* Angelica was a Colombian blonde he had found at a bookstore near Coral Gables. Talk to me Cupid, they fell in love like two twin flames. In that unquestionably Cuban nomenclature, Silvia had baptized her as *'La Lica'* after gossiping about her enough, and as the gossip developed and persisted, even the others began to refer to her as such — and the name stuck. So it was, *La Lica y El Tico. Casados. Cazados. Pero nunca cansados, porque será?* No, they were not yet married, but coupled enough to be referred to as *'Mari-novios'*, the Cuban merger of married and dating, the state between the two that in English could perhaps be called 'Matri-lationship.' To this day, Silvia considered Tico a gift from the Virgin, because he was the only one of her children that didn't drive her to the cigarettes every time they spoke...and he was born under the sign of Virgo. Silvia didn't believe in astrology though. Tico had a clean-shaven look, garnished with a thin, wispy moustache and a knack for wearing white. He grew Gardenias on his balcony for the sole purpose of wearing them on the lapel of his coat. His was a life of sweet bohemian oblivion: writing spiritual books for 'The Movement' as he called it, lounging, laughing, making too much love, with the whole world it seemed…and too much *café*.

20

"That kid, he'll never know what hard work is," said Chiche. "Never lifted a finger in his life, only to type his little books, his *libritos*." Chiche tipped the mug back and finished his *café con leche* with a smack of his lips. It was buttery from dipping the bread into it, and it always made him a little bloated in the afternoons, but he had grown to like the feeling. It was secure. He made the noise he always made in idle moments like these, the sort you make when you're picking at something in your teeth and the seal on your lips breaks. *Tss.* He hated it, but he did it compulsively and it drove Silvia even crazier, which made him laugh...so it evened out. Unstoppable as his compulsions were, the only thing to do was laugh.

Tico, however, would have disagreed. He bored the family over and over again with his musings on the power of *el Intimo*, of incarnating your 'inner master' and myriad other preposterous things. He was raised just like Mariza and Jennifer, but had always tended towards poetry and classical *danzónes* by the Orquesta Aragón while the other two loved to go out into the street and dance to the *rumba* of the little *conjuntos* on the corners. In fact, Tico knew all of José Martí's poems by heart, and even Mariza knew *Los Zapatícos de Rosa* word for word just from listening to him recite it over and over again back when they lived together. "*Ay, que inspiración!*" he would say with his little five year-old smile every time he finished his melodramatic recitations: he would end up inevitably on the floor, weeping fitfully on his knees, twisted into contortions and feigning death, his little hands to his throat, his face taut with thespian passion, his heart a blaze that everyone mistook for fantasy. She would never tell him, but Mariza was glad she knew the poem, because José Martí was the foremost intellectual, political philosopher, warrior and poet in historical Cuba—the man truly lived up to the size of his forehead. And it was *huge*.

Mariza however…*Mariza* was a different story. She was just as 'romantic' as Tico, but it was…in a *different* way. Mariza lived in Cutler Ridge, which her parents pronounced *Culo'e Res,* roughly translated as Cow's Ass. She lived in Cow's Ass with her latest *Mari-novio* Ricardo, or *el pobre Juan,* as Chiche called him. Juan, however, was not his name. The term derived from an old song named *El Pobre Juan,* or Poor Juan, that for Chiche, summed up the situation the poor guy found himself in: Mariza's pinky-ring. He was a radio salesman who loved to show off what he did not have and was up to his clip-on tie in debt. Still, however, he had enough swagger in his step to convince Mariza and the general public that he was doing alright, though his credit card companies had enough interest on his head to raise a ripe Catholic family. Oh Mother Mary, he got no sleep at night. For the first watch he would tumble around Mariza's curves, and for the other half he'd stare at his spackled ceiling thinking about how he was going to keep her thinking he had money.

But she knew his situation, though — come on now, *a Cuban girl?* Even *he* probably knew she checked all of his accounts behind his back, and it made her love him that much more, that he tried so hard to please her. She'd never tell him, though…it kept the two of them on edge. This was the only way to keep a relationship alive, Mariza had come to see. A tenebrous wisdom it was, that of Mariza's manipulations. She knew all there was to know about exploiting men, about the good life, and of that little flickering thread that could be found in between the two — if you looked at it right — that evoked something in her chest that reminded her of love. Mariza, without knowing it, was an Alchemist, for she turned the lead of anxiety into the gold of attraction, but unfortunately for the parties involved it was all at Ricardo's expense…*pobre Juan!* It seemed that she picked up more than poetry from Tico.

"*Bueeeee!*" said Chiche with pursed lips. "Back to work.

I'll see you later. Need anything?" he asked.

"*Mmhmm* — Bring me some *platanos*, would you?"

"Ok *vieja, mi viejita, mi negrita,* I'll bring you seven, twelve, anything you want, that's what I'm here for. Oh," and he turned around, smiling through his tired eyes. "*Te quiero, mi amor.*" I love you.

"*Hmph.* Bring me my *pastelitos.*" Chiche put his uniform back on and took a cigarette from Silvia's little white and gold Marlboro box as he went out the door. Silvia made a distasteful face. "I've only got three left now. *I could kill him, I swear.*" She considered herself a true smoker because of this, because she always knew how many she had in her pack. If you lost count or didn't care because you smoked so many, you were an addict, and if you knew how many you had only because you smoked so few, you had not yet cultivated your relationship with tobacco to the point of love. But Silvia, she knew how many cigarettes she had in her pack because she *loved* each and every one, and this made her a true smoker, at least in her own regard. What's the difference between a lover and an addict, between lead and gold?

~*~

"*Ay,* Alberto, didn't I ask you to put a towel in the bathroom for me?" Angelica strolled into the kitchen before the ocean-view window, naked and dripping wet. A sexy, glistening silhouette against bright blue sky, an ocean extending into infinity, into unity. Into..."Al...*berto?*"

"*Ah? Ay, si, si,* I...forgot. Forgive me," he smiled, tilting his head to the side. "Can I help if I wanted to see your divine figure cast against the backdrop of the ocean? *Ay,* Angelica, *mi amor, mi canto, mi flor!* You slay me with the precious spear of Eros." The lithe, alluring chalice of Tico's devotion swung her hair around her shoulder, catching the thick wad in her hands. She wrung it out like an old shirt, spattering a deluge of water onto the pristine tiles.

"Clean it," said the flower, leaving little footprints with each defiant step back to the room. Alberto lifted his demitasse to thin lips, taking another sip of *café* as he stared into the sunlight playing off of her footprints. She slept in most mornings; he encouraged her, saying that it was of the Goddess' nature to feel rested and pampered. But what he truly treasured was that he got to spend some time alone. It is very hard, you see, to convince a Latin woman that you still liked being with her while wanting to spend some time alone—"Well...why can't you spend some time alone with *me?*" It never went well, but this little loophole, their morning routine, was simply splendid. He let her sleep in to her heart's content, and in the meantime got to write in peace, or sit in absorption...just something quiet!

'The silence between the notes...it is the true music, my love.'

He appraised the situation pertaining to the water on the floor quietly from his stool. The room was spacious and clean, furnished with white walls that complemented the white furniture nicely, and the white kitchen appliances added a touch of elegance to the white carpet that was nearby in the living room, which of course, was decorated with various motifs that played on splashes of white. Great white tiles, 2 feet by 2 feet, lay across the kitchen floor, and they remained immaculately clean, save for the splatter that Angelica had left him while drying herself off.

"One of those white towels should do it, no? Hmm, well, I deserved it. Divine Mother! Eradicate my irresponsibility." Tico might have been an intellectual, but he was quite forgetful, entertained if you may, and it was not that he couldn't actually remember things, but that he was more often engrossed in the lofty thoughts that inspired his creative vision and helped him whet the knife of his wits. It cost him in certain aspects of his life, however, like conversing with his beloved, obeying traffic laws, remembering whether or not he locked the door, et cetera, et cetera. As a self-proclaimed Kabbalist who practiced unbroken awareness, this was an obvious burden to his quest, but it all worked out in the end. He needed to muse a little, he figured, in order to let his muse speak to him.

> *'Ay, and the sun looks so beautiful today, no?*
> *Lovers climax on the beach as we speak.'*

He went to the countertop and spun a mango in his hands before giving the golden-green heart a soft kiss and biting the tip, exposing a hint of its ambrosial flesh. He watched the tiny waves break far off in the world below. *All is energy in the ocean of consciousness.* The smell of last night's food lingered in the kitchen, and this brought impressions of his mother Silvia to his mind. *An intuition, I smell...* You see, Angelica had taken it upon herself to learn how to cook some of the foods she saw around Miami — if anything, to please a romantic soul so bad at hiding his preferences — and though Tico appreciated it, Silvia would always comment on it, on the fact that *La Lica* was irrevocably Colombian. *'Una Colommmbiana,'* she would say, slandering the words with a subtle grimace, *'cooking vacafrita — vaya, San Juan a baja'o su santísimo dedo.'* Tico was beyond it, though. He understood where his mother came from. 'It is an old way of Latin life,' he wrote in his notebook, 'a fact, in the way that rumors are facts, that all of us children of the Americas resent each other to a certain extent.' *Brilliant, brilliant.* 'Not in a real, destructive way, but in the way one would spurn a sibling, for being snot-nosed, more popular, unfair. Brotherly love, sisterly hate, it was simply family business.' Because of this, Tico would never tell his mother about the wonderful Colombian dishes Angelica cooked for him more often than not. Imagine, *imagínate*, a Cuban-born primogenitor on a predominantly Colombian diet? His Spanish would improve! Of course, it slipped over the phone once, by chance, and Silvia *pounced* upon the opportunity, leaving her response as a trademark quote for the way she felt about Angelica:

"Oh *si, mijito?* Well go ahead and eat all the *Bollo de Pescado* you want. I'm just fine over here with my *Ajiaco* and my sweet *café*." In Cuba, and hopefully not in Colombia, *'bollo'* was the term for that special part of a woman that should never taste like *pescado. Ay!* Precisely.

"Oh, you peeled me a mango?" Angelica came out wrapped in a towel, her hair swirled into another atop her head. She grabbed Tico's hand and raised it to her mouth, giving the mango a soft kiss before taking a juicy bite that splattered nectar onto the floor between them. Kissed him. She smiled into his eyes, wiping the juice from her chin. "*Ay*, it's perfectly ripe. Take a bite, no?" The *romantico* feigned contempt, licking his lips as she walked over to the glass pane once again, staring off into the ocean. Admiring her figure, he gave the mango a passionate bite, enjoying the suction it made when he bit into it. *Kissing and eating mangoes, the difference is in the lip of the beholder.* With a snap of his fingers, the towel fell from its place around Angelica, and she turned back to him with a *hmph*, cupping her hands where it mattered most. *Bingo, linda.* The towel fell onto the splatter from before.

"I've been inspired to write a verse this morning, would you like to hear it?" *I've written it for you...*"It's for you." *I tell you...*Lica only liked his poetry when it was for her.

"*Si, claro, amorsito.* Let me hear it," she smiled, unwrapping the towel from her hair. She wrapped it around her body, scoffing playfully. Tico cleared his throat, looking her over once before setting the mango down and grabbing the notebook next to him on the counter:

> This feeling tosses me all over
> Like a reckless ocean
> Flooding my heart with bliss
> And churning my mind with
> A mixture of all emotions

I am the happiest griever
The loneliest friend
The ugliest beauty
The most ignorant lover
That ever was,
A drunken scholar,
A sobered fool.

Blind
I am blind, blind bliss!
Unfurling itself like a flower
Everything that there ever was, is, or shall be

There is only love, and it is this flood
Beyond all, in all, of all
And I am all, this freedom
Found in the shackles of slavery
To another, to my only Self,
Resplendent in all, in you, in me,
And I am in love with everything,
With you, Angelica.

"*Ay, Alberto, I love it!*" Mischief flared in her deep, Colombian eyes. "...But you could have put anyone's name at the end of it...no?" He stared into two bottomless cups of coffee, *they will burn you if you're not careful! Son of Ibis, what a beautiful poem that would be.* Fortunately for all parties involved, drinking coffee was what Tico did best. Those who knew him well enough said that Alberto Campos could trick any woman into thinking she was a Goddess by the way he looked into her eyes. In truth, however, the trick was in making them think it was a game that he played.

"*Lica, Lica, mi amorsito!* But I put *your* name there! Yours alone, for I too am yours alone! Come here, *mi tocinillo del cielo,*" and he grabbed both of her busy hands, kissing her chest as she reeled back with laughter and ran back to the bedroom. Tico, too, had given into the name for Angelica. It was like most names in

27

Cuban households — a sort of joke.

"What shall we do today, then, *mi amor, hmmm?*" he shouted across the space. He sunk his teeth into the mango once again. Angelica paused in the room, tilting her head to the side with a coquettish squint.

"Let's go to the beach," she suggested. "The water is so beautiful today, did you see?"

"The beach…" Tico grimaced. "*No, no,* we go there too often. And I don't feel like I need to be any darker than I am already. Remember, love, we are Latinos, but of the European pedigree. I may not sunburn, but I look better when I am not bronzed," and he smirked, "or greased, with sunscreen." He passed a hand over the white lapel of his coat. "Besides, too much sun isn't good for us spiritual beings, it can rouse delirium. We thrive on grace, on doing everything in harmony with the Glorian." Angelica rolled her eyes. He wandered off into his thoughts for a second. "Right?" There was no response. "We should actually go *do* something, ah? Something beautiful, something exhilarating. Something that will make us forget that we are mortals…but not making love," he winked. "I want to go outside." He took another bite of the mango.

"Oh Tico, going outside does not change much for me when it comes to making love." Tico's heart went pink. "You know that." He looked down, suddenly uneasy. More nectar had dripped onto the floor. Setting a petite luncheon napkin underneath the mango, he checked himself over twice, assuring that he had not gotten any on himself…on his white suit.

"There is a responsibility that comes with wearing white, Angelica," he said, brushing the lapel of his coat. She rolled her eyes into the depths of her closet. "Not a choice, not a right, but a privilege it is, *certainly.* Assuming it upon oneself, one must take care to do everything with grace, with purpose, with elegance." *Brilliant, brilliant!* "Any mistakes show themselves clearly on the white suit, be it a stain or a scuff, any sign of clumsiness. Thus, those who can wear white must do it well, perfectly — inspired — for it becomes evident that anything that does not hold up to this standard approaches black, and this is clearly unsuitable."

"Why don't we go to visit your mother?" shouted Angelica from the bedroom. *There it is, intuitive one!* "I'm sure she could use the company."

"You know what? That...is an *excellent* idea," he answered, more to himself than to his beloved. "You must have read my thoughts, we become sensitive to that sort of thing, the closer we get." The Goddess with the rolling eyes. "I was just thinking of her, you see. Let us go later, though," he added, cracking a smile. "For some dinner, no?" Over in the bedroom, Angelica smiled as well. One tick off the to-do list. "I'll give her a call and let her know." He set the mango down on the counter, atop the luncheon napkin. "Until then, perhaps," he said, "why don't we go down to 8th, see what Augustín is doing, hmm?"

Angelica walked back into the kitchen. Her aura glowed in the bright sky behind her as she cocked an eyebrow and said, "There are only two things a man like him would be doing right now, and by the color of the sky, I feel like he is probably doing both — playing dominoes, and drinking *Havana Club Siete Añejo*."

"Well yes, but...I suppose...I wanted to...we should go talk to him, have a *coladita,* see what's going on down on *calle ocho,* you know? And," he grinned, "I'm pretty sure Manolito and Rogelio are back from Cuba..." Rolling eyes. "Well you know, I want to see if they brought me that *guiro* I asked them for." For the past three years or so he'd been after a specific *guiro* that Crispín Garcia made by hand in his workshop outside of Old Havana. It was perfectly crafted, made of the finest palm wood and shaped like a red snapper, the kind you fish off the coast when the days are long. As Angelica had commented to herself, the things sounded like a bullfrog getting squeezed to death from the bottom-up — *rrrrrrrrrrruueeeeeck-rrrrrickirrrrrruuuuueeeeeck!* But she couldn't help but like it, however, that sound, who didn't? It was oddly beautiful, the sort of Afro-Latin overtone that aroused the ear to the brink of assault with its deceptively simple repertoire. Sounds like these, in proper combination, were the type that drove people to dance their musically-induced tension off with huffing breaths and hot beads of sweat across their brows, *que rrrrrumba!* Tico's friends had finally remembered to ask the venerable Crispín Garcia to make him one last time they went, and with any luck, they would have brought it back with them on this last trip they made to Cuba. They went often, their bags full for both legs of the journey.

"Lica…" he said, "you've gone into your own head, you haven't answered me. That's bad for the consciousness." She swallowed her angst, lest it linger. "Does that sound like a plan, then?" She agreed tritely. *"Bueno!"* he sang, and hopped off the white stool by the counter. He walked across the kitchen and opened the glass door next to Angelica, walking by as if she didn't exist. He was headed to his Gardenias to perform his daily ritual with the flowers. "Let's get ready then," he said, his eyes fixed on the spritely bush that flourished all alone on the balcony. He spoke to each of the blossoms, asking which wanted to go with him that day. Angelica had no idea of the specifics involved, but apparently one of them told him that it was most fit to go on with him that given day, and he would pick it off the bush, letting the fragrance fill his aura until he disrobed and got into bed. At first she didn't believe him, but to assert his integrity over the matter he insisted that she choose the flower for him once. As one can imagine, it had shriveled by mid-morning in the heat of the day, and Tico threw it away, making a show of it in front of her and their friends at the *café*. The ones *he* picked stayed perfectly white all day. Unless they were red, of course, but the essence of the matter is beyond such triviality. *Delicious.*

The Goddess with the rolling eyes.

She watched as he turned to each blossom, caressing them

slowly, singing to them, asking them which wanted to come along to see Augustín, and after cocking his ear towards a few of them, nodding or squinting his eyes with an interest too tangible for fabrication or even psychosis, he gave one of them a long kiss and picked it from the little bush, nodding as if responding to a cue. He fixed it to the lapel of his coat and walked back inside, moving towards his shoes, a pair of pristine two-toned *Luc-Marniers* he had his cousin Manolito send him from *Lissette's* in Havana. They were off-white and tan, featuring elegant laces tipped with tin aglets plated with 24-karat gold. More like dessert than footwear. Angelica agreed, indeed, she thought they were the most beautiful shoes she had ever seen for a man, but she never let Albertico know. Not because she didn't want to, but because he would undoubtedly take offense to the whole thing.

You see, Tico had expressed one too many times that he never wanted to receive compliments, for explicitly spiritual reasons. If she wanted to compliment something, the shoes for example, she should compliment the item in question as opposed to the one who donned them in the given moment. Such a thing was only proper, he would say with his prrrretentious lips, it would ultimately help him in his quest to complete the great psychological work of destroying the ego. As much as she wished he would drop the whole thing, she went along with his ploys because there was nothing in the world more dear to her than the way he looked into her eyes. She smiled as he laced them slowly, delightfully engrossed in the task. He put on his hat, his coat, and buttoned his shirt to the second button, just below the pit in his neck, and only then did he venture a gaze towards Angelica.

"Are you going in that towel? It's hardly appropriate, *vamonos mi amor!*" Lica scurried off into the other room, slightly embarrassed by the moment she had lost in an idle stare, and got dressed for an afternoon on 8th street, right in the heart of Little Havana. But she needed to be dressed for dinner too. Fancy? No, but presentable. Who will be there? Will they care? Will I sweat?

Will they judge me for it?
> *Should I even care?*
> *Did I just break awareness?*
> *Am I not aware of breaking awareness?*

> *"Am I going freaking nuts?"*

The questions floated around her as she pecked shoulder after shoulder of her dresses, blouses, tops, outfits, blue, yellow, white, off-white, cream, peach, green — *ni modo!* — and oh, this one looks perfect. What *will* I walk into tonight at their house, anyway? There, the food was secondary…she could see it now. Whoever was there would sit at the table, tease Tico for not eating pork, you gotta be *born* Jewish, just take a bite Tico el Bambino, make fun of Colombians for a bit — in good spirits, of course — and then they would all sit for a generous smattering of Silvia's infamous cuisine. Dinner at Silvia's house was almost spiritual, a temple for the forlorn palate, an excruciating test of initiation for any locus of consciousness in search of sensor-emotional equipoise. *Ah, that was nice, little bird.* Her food had a certain something to it that was almost…unpleasant, but it was precisely this that made it so beautiful, a secondhand buzz, making you eat until well past full. One could find 'home-cooked' Cuban food at every *timbiriche* in Miami, but at Silvia's house you always came home to a hot plate of that look in her eyes, affection and lady-like dignity tinged with the slightest hint of disdain. It was…an affair without the sex. *Ay Magdalena,* she thought to herself, *I'm beginning to sound like Tico.*

She cocked her head up — "Isn't…isn't that love?"

"Mami? Mami? Si, si…we're coming over tonight, we…*mmhmm, mmhmm…rrrrropavieja? Ay si!* We'll see you at six. I'll bring you a tin of *guayaba*…you know, the kind you like…*ay, coñitos,* why can't I ever make you a surprise! *Si, si, te quiero mucho* *muah!* *adios, mi madre divina, que vayas con*

"As we knew your measurements, I took the liberty of purchasing some clothing for you." She glanced at me, "I hope you will like what I selected."

"Thanks," I said gratefully. "It will be nice to have clothes other than borrowed military uniforms. Lots of grey in my wardrobe at the moment."

She laughed her pretty laugh. "I assure you, I bought only colors I felt would complement and support you through your adjustments."

I wondered to myself what colors those could be, not convinced anything other than time could really help me. Or therapy, I supposed. However, I loved the blue of the robe I was wearing. It was very calming, like the ocean on a warm, sunny day.

Domena had opened another door off of my room and gestured for me to follow. I found myself in an ultra-modern bathroom. She showed me how to use the various fixtures' operating panels, and fortunately, they were pretty straightforward and easy to follow. After the two-minute showers on the space station, the idea of indulging myself in a long bath was a temptation I couldn't resist.

"I'll leave you to refreshen," Domena said with a smile. "I well understand that look of yearning. The first thing I did when we arrived on the planet was to take a bath, using as much hot water as I wanted."

I grinned. "There's not much of that on any space station, I'll warrant."

"Sadly, no," she replied. "Mind you, we did have a family soaking tub, but it's not the same as shutting yourself off from little boys and totally relaxing." She headed toward the door, pausing before she left me to my privacy. "When you are ready, just walk down the hallway to your left and you will find our common room and the kitchen beyond."

The bath was heavenly, although I was mindful not to take too long. I had to promise myself I'd take another at bedtime before I reluctantly hauled myself up out of its warmth. Thanks to super-duper technology, the water never got cold. Just blissful. When I slid open the closet, I was presented with a rainbow of pastel colors. I felt a smile tugging at the corners of my mouth. *A wardrobe for a movie star*, I thought, going through all the different choices, feeling the fabrics between my fingers and lingering over some. I finally selected a filmy, blousy apricot top with matching pants that floated around me when I moved. There were soft little shoes that matched exactly among several selections neatly lined up on the closet floor. I found some underwear in a drawer built into the closet's wall and hastily dressed.

The common room was in keeping with the rest of the home's open floor plan. There were a few toys clumped haphazardly under a table standing against a wall, giving it a lived-in quality and a pop of color. Otherwise the room was pretty neutral—taupe and tan with slate blue and forest green accents. A series of glass panels looked out onto the back yard and the hills beyond. I wondered if Bren's cabin was in those hills. I'd know soon enough, I supposed.

But for now, I followed my nose to the kitchen, where I found Domena arranging a variety of fruit and breads on a turquoise-trimmed plate.

"How pretty," I murmured.

She glanced up with a smile. "Do you like my arrangement of your breakfast?" she asked.

"Very much," I said, and my stomach growled. I clutched my stomach, feeling my cheeks heat up.

Domena laughed. "I do believe we should waste no time and get you settled in front of this plate." She inclined her head toward a table set beyond a half-wall partition.

As I followed her, I took a quick look at the kitchen. The appliances looked similar enough I was pretty sure I could whip something up in there myself. Interesting, I thought, how familiar things could be when you thought about how they were meant to be used. It would be like cooking in Europe versus cooking in America—differences were doable. Nice. I felt myself relaxing just a fraction.

I sat down in front of my plate, leaning forward to appreciate its artistry. Domena sat across from me with an identical plate. She had placed a teapot of something between us, steam gently swirling out of its mouthpiece.

"Is that tea?" I asked.

She nodded. "Ian has been doing some research on your home planet. I thought you might appreciate something that felt like home." She lifted the pot and poured the steaming beverage into a mug, which she passed to me.

I sniffed at the aromatic blend. It was unfamiliar but reminded me a little of a spiced maté.

We ate in silence, both of us taking the time to slowly savor the meal. The fruit was juicy and sweet. The bread was dark and savory, a nice blending of flavors and textures.

I sat back, wiping the juice from my fingers on a napkin.

"That was absolutely delicious," I pronounced.

Domena beamed. "I'm happy you enjoyed it."

She rose and took my plate as I refilled our tea mugs. I heard her rinsing dishes in the sink. Not so different from home, I thought.

Returning, Domena sat and studied me for a few moments.

"You seem more alert now."

"I am," I nodded. "I'm feeling much better, actually, since I slept so well. And the bath was amazing!" I hesitated. "But I have to be honest, I am feeling very awkward and inept. I don't know how to behave properly. I'm afraid I will ignorantly make some huge slip up in the social arena. You see," I said, leaning forward, "I wrote about your military, so I can sort of function knowledgably in that arena. But visiting people? Social calls?" I shrugged. "I feel like I'm a faux pas waiting to happen."

Domena smiled and shook her head, her glorious hair flowing about her. "No need to worry about that. We are a civilization built from an ever-increasing number of different cultures. If there is a rule for being in society, it would to be open-minded and accepting. It is the only way for us all to coexist. Please, Rose, this time is for you. Just relax. Ian and I enjoy all the different species of sentients. Both of us are intrigued by the many varieties of cultures."

I stroked the fabric on my sleeve. "Thank you," I said, looking up. "You have been so kind to me already. I just wanted to get it out in the open. If I appear rigid or stiff, that's why."

"Then I will be open-minded and accepting. Are we in agreement?" she asked with a smile.

I nodded and smiled in return. "Yes, we are in agreement."

She nodded with a satisfied smile. "So tell me, Rose, why do you think you are here?"

I shrugged, not sure how much she knew about me, other than my being a 3rd. If her boys knew, then it wasn't a very big secret. "Ian invited me," I answered. "I'm assuming you know my, uh, history. I'm trying to get over the shock of it all and get back to some semblance of normal. Ian thought if I rested in a semi-familiar environment, it might be easier for me to adapt."

"Ahhh," she said nodding slightly, "I thought that was the case."

I set down my mug. "What do you mean?"

"This was all Brennar's design."

"Bren's? Then why didn't he tell me?"

"Because, I suppose, he very much wanted you to come here."

I cocked my head at her, "I'm not understanding."

"Tell me, Rose, would you have so easily complied if the invitation had come from Brennar?"

I went very still and felt that telltale warmth of embarrassment flushing my face. "No," I admitted, "Probably not. I would have felt I was imposing."

Domena reached across the table and gently touched my hand. "Brennar has very deep feelings for you, Rose," she said quietly. "He thought it might help you assimilate your recent experiences if you could talk with someone outside of the military. Especially," she added, "if that someone were also an artist. As artists and women, we can more easily find common ground."

She paused and in the silence, I could hear soft, peaceful music.

"Rose, this galaxy is vast, as you are well aware. My home planet is light years away from Montorea, and even further from Astragon 7, where I went to become a Harmonist. I can remember the loss and disquiet I felt when I first arrived. I was desperate to talk to someone. I can't begin to imagine how much more difficult these experiences are for you, especially since you were removed from a life you knew and enjoyed in such a tragic and dramatic fashion."

I ducked my head when I felt the tears began to form. There was just something about her sincerity that went right through all my mental barriers.

Domena squeezed my hand. "I am a very good listener, my dear," she told me gently. "It is who I am and what I do."

In the silence, I listened to the soothing music and squeezed Domena's hand back, taking the time I needed to regroup. I hate asking for help. I took a deep breath, swiped at my face and then looked up. "Thank you," I said, sniffling a bit. "Bren was right. I really need to spend peaceful time with someone outside of the military, with all their danged protocols and short showers."

She chuckled and stood. "I have a home office with two very comfortable chairs. Shall we make use of them?"

I nodded and smiled back, grateful she was allowing me a little time to compose myself.

"Then follow me."

She handed me my mug, picked up her own and, with

the teapot in her other hand, led me down another corridor and up a short flight of stairs to a landing with two doors, one with a jeweled doorknob.

"This is my inner sanctum," she told me, opening the door with the jeweled knob and ushering me in. "Far away from the boys' playroom. Ian's office is across the landing." She chuckled. "It is one reason we chose this particular home. We love our boys, but there are times we need to work here, and they can make concentration a challenge."

I nodded. "Your boys appear to be quite lively."

"Lively, delightful and loud," Domena said with a soft smile, the smile of a woman who loves being a mother.

The room was just like Domena, elegant and welcoming, with exquisite pieces of art placed thoughtfully about. The honey-colored chair I sank into was as comfortable as promised. A small, circular ottoman placed between the two chairs mirrored their rounded backs and served as a coffee table. Its effect was intimate and cozy. I took another sip of my tea and set it down on the ottoman.

"This is nice," I said, settling in with a sigh.

"I often come here simply to enjoy these chairs," Domena confided. "And the view of the hills," she added. "I am told Brennar's cabin is in those hills."

"I was wondering about that earlier," I told her peering out the window. "Have you ever been there?"

She shook her head. "I have heard it is quite rustic," she answered, and then added with a chuckle. "It would be a Harmonist's dream to play with the raw material a rustic cabin offers."

"No doubt," I said with a laugh. Then I took a deep

breath. "But that is neither here nor there at the moment, is it?" I said soberly.

"Oh but it is! We are learning about one another. Is that not how a friendship begins on Earth? You are such a fascinating and interesting individual, Rose. I would enjoy developing a friendship with you. Especially," she added, "since you are so important to one of my family."

"Brennar," I said.

"Brennar," she agreed. "You must know how special you are to him," she said with a smile. "When it comes to you his feelings are quite, quite transparent."

I grinned back. "With that mem-unit of his strapped to my head for several hours, yes, I did gather he considers me special for a number of reasons...and that's the problem."

"How can it be a problem? A handsome, strong, and sensitive man who would do anything for you?"

I laughed, "Well, if you put it that way..." And then I sobered, hoping she would understand.

"It frightens me, you see. I actually loved Joss, the character in my novels. No man could measure up to the character I created. I thought I was losing my mind at one point, because I would rather write about Joss than date a real man. But, now I see Joss was actually Bren, and quantum entanglement meant it wasn't as crazy as I'd thought, falling for a fictitious character. I understand that now."

I held up a finger to forestall Domena's comment.

"However," I continued, "Joss is Bren filtered through my perceptions. So, who am I really loving? Is it Bren, or is it who I believe Bren to be? And then there's the slight problem of trusting my instincts after what happened just before Bren came to my rescue."

Domena raised an eyebrow in what I was learning was a classic Domena move.

I considered her.

"Heck, I may as well tell you all, since I've started," I exclaimed, brushing my hair back, "Otherwise you may not understand my confusion."

"Before Bren rescued me, I was betrayed by Sam, a man with whom I had recently become involved, and who, incidentally, surprise-surprise," I said sarcastically, "I met because he was the winner of the Joss Walker, Emissary of Evolution Look-Alike Contest. It was Sam who turned me over to the bad guys. I'm still reeling from that."

"Of course you are, dear," Domena said, compassion radiating from her eyes.

I swallowed.

"I know, right?" I said, after a moment.

Domena nodded.

"And then, as if my emotions aren't scrambled enough," I continued, "I thought I had died. But I had actually been revived and my essence poured into an immortal body, and there is only one other like it in the whole Universe." I looked at her, "And we both know who's living in the other one."

I flung my arms out. "I'm a mess." I told her with a short little laugh.

I knew if I weren't careful, I'd end up in tears again.

"I can see how you might be experiencing a little bit of

confusion," Domena replied with just enough levity in her voice to help me regain my balance.

I snorted and reached for my tea.

She reached out and touched my hand. "Before you continue with your explanations, I feel compelled to tell you Ian has already told me much of your history. I hope that doesn't trouble you," she said worriedly.

I did not answer her immediately.

"I am a private person, Domena," I explained slowly, "But I do understand why Ian would discuss me with you. After all, I am a virtual stranger you have invited into your home," I paused, "and you are helping me re-gather."

"Thank you for your forgiveness," she said sincerely, withdrawing her hand.

We both took sips of tea, buying a little time to settle back into comfort.

"You do realize," she began gently, setting her mug down, "Brennar experienced very similar conflicting emotions, learning to deal with his dreaming of you, his PeaceKeeper obligations, and the adjustments to his corpus. Of all sentients, he would be the best one for you to turn to."

I nodded miserably. "But I don't think I'm quite ready to tell a man who loves me I don't know who it is I am loving—the real man, or my imaginary man." I added, "And no matter how logically I approach all this, my experience with Sam has made me feel very jumpy and uncertain. I don't trust myself, let alone others."

"Do you really believe you could not trust Brennar?"

"Of course I can trust Brennar," I told her. "He reeks of

trustworthiness! But I know there is going to come a time in the not-too-distant-future Bren will want to be intimate." I hid my face in my hands, took a deep breath, and dropped my hands abruptly. "This is hard for me to say," I told her feeling my cheeks heat up again. "Like I said, I'm a private person.

"But, you see, all my new body wants to do is merge with Bren's body. They're made out of the same stuff, and apparently it recognizes that. It's like my body has a mind of its own. When Bren and I are together, I find myself reaching out just to connect with him. And that frightens me. I feel I have no control over my body *or* my feelings, and if we become intimate, I have no idea what I will become." I looked at her. "I know that makes no sense, but it's just one more thing that has been taken out of my hands. I didn't choose to house Bren's seed atoms. I didn't choose to entangle with Bren. I didn't choose to be kidnapped. I didn't choose for my soul to be placed in this body I cannot even control."

I looked at her helplessly.

She gazed back, calm and serene. I envied her.

"What do we ever decide?" she asked me. "We are each led by events and the choices we make because of them. Some argue sentients have free will. Others will argue all actions are a part of the ever-expanding Divine Design."

"What do you think?" I asked after I pondered her words.

"What I think, Rose, is it really does not matter how we arrive at the crossroads in our lives. I think what matters, is how we manage ourselves during times of discontent and, for that matter, during times of contentment, as well.

"Sentients are so complicated, are they not?" Domena

mused after a pause. "It is what makes us so interesting. Perhaps, if you thought about what Bren, not Joss, has done for you, how he has behaved since he brought you here," she suggested. "Could that help you separate the differences?"

I perked up because my inner problem-solver just kicked in, thank goodness. What Domena suggested was something I could do. "That's something I've not thought about," I told her. "I could begin a list of what I have noticed about Bren since I woke up in my new body. Not comparing him to Joss or even with what I know from the mem-unit experience."

"I suppose you might also make a list of how you feel when you are near Brennar, perhaps to learn to differentiate those feelings from your corpus' demands. Perhaps it will enable you to feel more in control."

I felt suddenly lighter. "Good suggestion. Thank you, Domena."

She bowed her head in acknowledgement. "As for adjusting to your new environment," she added, "how may I support your re-gathering?"

I took a sip of tea and shrugged. "Just listening to me, helping me sort through my feelings, has helped enormously. I honestly don't know what else you could do for me, other than distract me so my subconscious has time to sort it all out. I'm hoping I'll have a moment of enlightenment," I chuckled. "Would you like to help distract me?"

She laughed. "I believe the boys can help with distractions, as well."

"I can imagine your boys make excellent distractors," I said with a grin.

She nodded, half-closing her eyes like a contented cat. "Shall we allow your subconscious to begin its work, then? Would you like for me to distract you by telling you a bit about our Artisans?"

"Great idea!" I said. "I've been wondering, are there still writers, or has that craft evolved into something else?"

"We call writers Wordsmiths, and there are many kinds. Some, like you, write stories to entertain. These can be enhanced by combining the story with visuals and sounds in a number of ways."

Domena went on to describe what seemed like a combination of book/manga/live-action game and mini-movie all rolled into one, all orchestrated by the author. As soon as I started thinking about so many different ways to express a story, my creative juices started flowing. Perhaps it wouldn't be too bad living in an advanced society.

We talked all afternoon. There was so much to absorb, but instead of being overwhelming, Domena's descriptions made me curious and excited. Ian brought the two boys home close to dinnertime, and they entertained me with their very sophisticated toys and commiserated that the boys from Earth didn't have any toys nearly as exciting as theirs.

At bedtime, Domena showed me how to program my room to fit my sleep goals, be they resting, dreaming or problem-solving. After another long bath, I donned a nightgown and crawled into the bed. As I drifted off, I began to mentally list what Bren had done for me, starting with saving my life.

Over the next few days, I was happy to notice the Sleep Aid (as I called the room-programing mechanism on my bedroom wall) was beginning to have an effect. Too bad they didn't have this technology back on Earth for trauma victims, because I was adjusting far more rapidly. I no longer felt the need to run, hide, cry or deny. Instead, I felt more and more like my naturally optimistic self, ready to take on new situations and curious to find out more about my new environment and friends. I wanted to bow down and worship whoever created that contraption.

Over the weekend, I had the opportunity to watch Bren interact with his family when he joined us for a family picnic in a local park. Being able to observe him when he was relaxed and enjoying himself made some pretty deep inroads with my goal to separate what I'd witnessed with Bren's mem-unit memories, my body's wish to glom onto him, and my own thoughts and feelings.

I particularly loved watching him play with his nephews. He was so patient and sweet with them, a benevolent panther allowing cubs to crawl all over him. Watching this happy, easy-going Bren, I could much more easily imagine him pulling a prank like the ones described by Frankie.

It also gave me the opportunity to covertly admire Bren's physique. He was not tall, I'd say 2 or 3 inches below 6 feet. But his sleek muscles and the way he carried himself made me think he was tall. Nice, sleek panther muscles rippled under the tee shirt he was wearing. His sandy brown hair was an overgrown military cut and just beginning to curl. He had an oval face, slender, straight nose, full lower lip and a strong jaw. His eyes were an intense blue with a darker ring of blue around the edges. And even with mascara on, my lashes would never be as thick and sooty, dammit. Beautiful hands, too, with long tapering fingers. Panther paws.

That link of ours must have been humming because, just at that moment, he caught my eye from beneath a pileup of giggling boys. With that slow, sweet smile he sent me I felt my insides melt. Because Bren the Man had something Joss the Character did not. When he smiled, Bren had a dimple on his left cheek, low, near the jawline.

Why that would make such a huge difference to me, I did not know.

But it did.

Chapter 22 - The Cabin

Bren let go of my hand and I staggered. Again. "Man!" I told him, grabbing his arm for balance. "I thought I'd be more prepared this time. Anyway," I said, "It still beats waiting for a plane."

He grinned, flashing his single dimple. "The more I teleport, the more I appreciate it," he said.

I looked about the cabin, trying to separate my impressions from the memories I'd picked up from Bren. I discovered if I were in places I'd known from my dip into Bren's brain via the mem-unit, to get my own reactions, the best way was to look at the situation as if I were editing a scene from my novel. It helped immensely. I was rather proud of myself for discovering this mindset.

The cabin was small and rustic, with two bedrooms, a bath, and a kitchen and living/dining area. Not too different from ones I've stayed in on Earth. I relaxed, feeling curiosity getting a toehold in my super-duper Silistel brain.

"So," I said, scooping up the satchel full of my new colorful clothing Bren had carried along, "May I put my things in the second bedroom?" Since I was already heading towards that door, it was a rhetorical question.

I walked to the middle of the room and turned in a slow circle.

It was empty.

I set my satchel down in a corner and glanced at Bren, who now leaned casually against the doorframe.

"Have you ever teleported a bed?" I asked.

Bren smiled. "I think I am about to."

In a flash, he was non-existent.

I really wanted to learn that trick.

Bren reappeared with the bed I had used on Salinio 5. Oh, how I wished he'd brought the one I'd used at Ian's and Domena's home.

"Is that hard to do?" I marveled.

"It's about believing you can," he answered, positioning the bed against a wall. "If I could teleport myself, I knew I could teleport any inanimate object, despite its size." He flashed that irresistible dimple. "And I just finished bringing you and your clothing here."

I must have looked doubtful, because he added, "The first time is the hardest, Rose."

"Well, that's why we're here, isn't it? For us to see what our hybrid bodies can do?"

Bren nodded. "Would you like me to fetch other furnishings?"

"Yes, please," I replied. "A sitting chair, a table for next to the bed, a rug and some curtains. Oh, and a dresser for my clothes."

He frowned. "I will see what I can find from Sal 5, but I'm not sure I can provide all of it."

I smiled, "Maybe we can cobble it together from the rest of the cabin."

With a nod and a flash, Bren was gone again. In another flash, he was back with a chair and small table, again acquired from my room on Salinio 5. Looking about the cabin, we found a chest that would function as my dresser, and a spare rug that had been rolled up in one of the closets. The rug smelled musty, but I opened a window and it helped. We arranged my room and then stood back and admired it. Simple. Stark. Functional.

"Perhaps we can find other items in town," Bren suggested.

I shrugged. "Well, it's not as nice as the room I had at your brother's but it will do just fine."

He left me to unpack, which didn't take long. I followed the sound of running water and found Bren in the kitchen.

"I would think highly technologically advanced beings would have highly technologically advanced dwelling places," I said. "But this cabin is definitely not that. I could be back on Earth."

Bren turned towards me, wiping his hands on a towel he'd slung onto the sink. "It's all about preference, Rose," he explained. "We can choose how much or how little technology we want to live with. Is it not the same for you on Earth?"

I nodded. "Yes, but…" I shook my head. "I guess I never really thought about it," I said with a laugh. "Writing about advanced societies is very different from living in them."

"If it makes you feel any better, Rose, I feel much more at home on a ship or station up there," he said pointing upwards.

I smiled. "And I'm glad we're not up there," I said, pointing up. "I do believe I am a true Planet-Strider. Why don't you show me around outside? I'm feeling bold. I want to get familiar with this landscape."

"Very well, bold one, follow me," Bren said, reaching for my hand.

As usual, the contact gave me a little jolt of pleasure. As he led me outside, I wondered had I been back in my old body, if I'd have had the same reaction to his touch. And then I wondered what it would be like to kiss him. *That answers that*, I thought as I focused on damping down the glow, grateful for the distraction of the great outdoors.

Chapter 23 - Show Me What You've Got or Anything You Can Do...

The next few days quickly fell into a pattern.

As Bren had done following his first contact with the 9th, we simply lived.

We got up when the sun rose, took a run in the woods, followed by a dip in the lake. Then we ate breakfast and planned what we would practice that day.

"Let's take a walk," I suggested, as I put the last dish away and emptied the drain. "I want to see if I can talk to plants," I told him, drying my hands on my pants as I headed toward the door.

Bren lifted an eyebrow but followed me outside.

We both stood looking at a fern-like plant bordering his yard, both of us with our arms crossed.

"Now what?" he asked, tapping his fingers on his arm.

"I don't know," I shrugged. "Maybe just reach out to it like we reach out to each other. With our thoughts, you know?"

I closed my eyes and focused on the plant, open to whatever would happen, and waited. I waited in the stillness of the morning.

And then I heard it.

Music.

Like someone humming a little tune while they worked.

I opened my eyes and grinned at Bren.

"Did you hear it? It's singing as it's growing."

He shook his head. "I don't hear the song, but I see colors swirling around it."

"Show me," I told him, grasping his hand. Our fingers interlaced and he sent his impressions of what he saw through our link until I saw it, too.

I gasped.

Rainbows of energy moved between the plant and the sun, the plant and the earth, the plant and all the other plants surrounding it.

"It's beautiful," I whispered.

Through our connection, I returned the favor and shared with Bren the music I heard from the one plant. I began listening for others.

Bren glanced at me and shook his head in wonder. "I had no idea."

I don't know how long we stood there, soaking up the symphony of color and sound as it washed over us, when suddenly we both realized we had become a part of it. The plant was sending rainbows to us. Then our corpuses began sending rainbows in return. I felt I was dissolving into the whole experience, and it was wonderful and magical.

And then I realized I was unraveling. I didn't know where I began and the rest of the world left off. It scared me shitless.

I let go of Bren's hand and fled into the cabin. Scrambling onto the couch, I wrapped my arms tight about me. If there had been a blanket handy, I would have hidden beneath it.

Bren had followed me in, his expression mixed with concern and surprise.

"I got scared," I told him in a small voice.

"Of what, Rose?"

"Of losing myself. I thought I was going to just dissolve into it and be nothing and everything at once."

I shivered.

"As a 9th," he answered, "That is the joy of being a 9th." He sat beside me and took my hand. "I felt the same way, Rose, only it was not frightening to me. Not at all. It was liberating. It was empowering. I felt as if I belonged to everything and everything belonged to me."

I shivered again. "It felt to me like dying. Like being no more. Like if I dissolved so completely, I'd never find my way back together again."

Bren drew me close, and I huddled into his warmth, feeling the weight of his chin on my head. His chin. My head. Two different things.

I could deal with that.

"I know you, Rose," Bren spoke softly. "You would find your way back together again."

I sighed, not nearly convinced. "Perhaps I should just table the plant communication idea for a little while longer."

"What if we focused on communicating with each other, then?" he suggested. "Does that make you feel lost?"

I withdrew from his embrace to look at him. "Not really," I said slowly, "I guess because our bodies are made from the same stuff, and we've been doing it from the get-go. And," I added, "If it got to be too much, I know you'd stop. I don't know if a plant would, or could."

"Then why don't you take a short break while I check in with the League? When I return, we can begin again."

I nodded. "Sounds good," I said and added a mock salute to see if I could get his dimple to flash when he smiled.

It worked.

* * *

Both of us were fascinated with how the two of us could communicate on so many simultaneous levels. Not wanting to push myself beyond my comfort levels, that is usually what we would end up doing--practicing our communication skills--how to mask our thoughts for privacy, how to send images to one another by touch or by thought, how to stop that telling glow.

We discovered when we touched one another with the intention of transferring knowledge, it felt very much like downloading to a mem-unit. Once we discovered that means of knowledge transference, as Bren called it, it enabled us to share vast quantities of information. I learned several languages, including the expletives. Bren learned some

English expletives, how to drive a car, read a GPS system and a road map. You would think he would have an easy time with mechanical things, but his technologies were so advanced it was difficult for him to recognize anything familiar as a starting point.

I remember a conversation from my Bren mem-unit experience, when he had talked about piloting a low-tech aircraft, and my admiration for him grew. I had had a hard enough time switching to a different computer operating system when I'd bought a MacBook.

We practiced until we were hungry. When hungry, we made lunch. Following lunch, we would exercise some more. I took Bren through my martial arts katas. He caught on quickly, and soon we were sparring. Since we could read one another's thoughts, we weren't able to use the element of surprise, so we turned our sparring into games of speed and dexterity.

It was during one of these sparring matches I first teleported. I imagined I was behind him and…there I was.

It really was that easy.

With a whoop, I jumped on his back, and when he was about to throw me I teleported across the yard, laughing as he stumbled. He looked at me wickedly, and suddenly I was wrapped in his arms. I put myself on the dock, thinking I was safe, and dropped my guard.

Suddenly I was in Bren's arms again, in a flying tackle throwing us right into the water. I shrieked and sputtered.

"Uncle! Uncle!" I shouted, shaking the water from my eyes.

He looked at me quizzically.

"I thought you learned English," I laughed, dunking him again before teleporting for towels.

We stood together in the sunshine, toweling off.

It felt like a good moment to introduce an idea I'd been toying with, especially since I'd just learned to teleport.

"Bren?" I began.

"Yes, Rose?" he answered with a grin, still caught up in our antics.

"I want to go to my home."

He stopped toweling to look at me. Then he touched me, sending images of what it took to organize the first scouting mission to an Awakening planet.

I shook my head. "No, not like that," I told him. "Just a quick visit. Just to see what happened to my home. My things." I touched him so he could understand my yearning, the need to know what had happened. Did Lacy think I was dead? How had my disappearance been explained?

"We cannot contact anyone," he warned, knowing where my thoughts were heading. I nodded with a sigh.

"We go together, Rose."

I sensed his concern for my safety without him touching me.

"Okay," I agreed, "we go together. But I'm eternal. They can't hurt me, Bren, not really."

"And how can we be sure you have fully harmonized with your corpus?" he asked.

I bowed my head. He was right. He had lived in his longer than I had lived in mine.

"We go after we are dry," he said abruptly, and then smiled. "I want to see Earth. I want to see your birth planet, Rose, probably as much as you want to see Astragon 7."

Would I ever get used to the way he looked at me?

I shivered.

* * *

To my surprise, it was just as easy to teleport across the stars as it was to teleport across the yard in front of Bren's cabin. I blinked and let out a little laugh when I saw we were standing in my living room. I moved to my bay window and opened the blinds, sneezing when the dust tickled my sensitive nose.

It was night, and the city lights spilled into the room. I heard the distant hum of traffic and the occasional honk of a car horn. As my eyes adjusted, my delight vanished.

We stood in the middle of a crime scene straight out of television show. Everywhere I looked I saw fingerprint dust and yellow tape. I froze when I saw the outline of a body and what I assumed was dried blood on my favorite oriental carpet.

"So they killed me off," I said to Bren, feeling the anger building deep within my belly.

"It appears so," he replied, scanning the area.

His light touch was soothing.

I crossed over to my desk, Bren close behind, but allowing me the space I needed just then.

Sure enough, my laptop was gone, as was the filing cabinet where I kept my outlines and bits of dialogue for future novels. Anger surged through me again and I headed into my bedroom.

It looked like it had been hit by a hurricane. *So much for respecting the dead,* I thought. Drawers were half opened with clothes spilling out, more fingerprint dust, the bedclothes pulled and stripped back from the bed. I went to my jewelry box on the dresser to see what was left.

Nothing of value remained. I smiled. Nothing but my most prized possession, that is. I slipped the braided bracelet my dad had made from paracord onto my wrist, hearing him once again tell me how important it was to always have extra when out in the wilderness, just in case.

With a sigh, I turned to the closet and picked up a duffle bag that had been carelessly flung on the floor. Since it was already unzipped, I began sifting through my clothes, finding my favorites.

"This will take just a minute," I told Bren, who stood silently in the doorway.

"Who's that?" he asked, scowling at the cardboard statue of Joss.

"Don't you recognize yourself? It's Joss, my character." I laughed and waved him over to it. "Go stand by him so I can compare."

"What is it doing in your bedroom?" he asked as he begrudgingly walked over to stand by the model.

"Not telling," I answered primly. I fluttered my hand at him, "Go on, assume the Joss stance."

He did and I just stood there shaking my head.

"You two look an awful lot alike, I must say," I told him. "I do believe I would have picked you as the winner to the contest."

His scowl deepened and he turned to face the model. "*This* looks like me? No, Rose. This is a cardboard image of some sentient pretending to be something he is not. This cannot possibly look like me."

I cocked my head and looked at them both again. "I'm sorry, Bren, but that is, indeed, what you look like. You two are identical, like looking in a mirror." I looked at Bren and started to grin. "I do believe I've made you glow!"

"I am not glowing,"

"Yes, you are. It's a glower glow." I started to laugh.

"I'm not seeing the humor." He was still glowering, but he'd banked the glow.

"I know," I chuckled. "That makes it even funnier. I do believe you are a little jealous of Joss."

He shook his head. "I am not jealous of a," he gestured at the cardboard figure, "*that*. Why is it not in the living space? Wouldn't it be more appropriate there?"

I laughed again.

He frowned but I swore his lips twitched. "Will you bring him with you along with other belongings?"

"Well, it would make the cabin feel more like home."

My good humor was catching. He started to smile. "Mac would appreciate it."

I nodded.

"Why don't you and Joss go into the other room so I can focus on what I want to bring with me?"

I laughed at how he carried him out, slung over his

shoulder. And then sobered pretty quickly. There was so much I would have liked to bring.

I began to dig around in my closet, looking for my favorite pair of black lace Jimmy Choos. I reverently put them in my bag. And, since I had the shoes, I might as well bring out the little black dress. Just as reverently, I drew it from my closet, a little strapless number with a black lace bodice still in its dry-cleaning plastic. I carefully rolled it up and placed it in the duffle next to the shoes.

When I collected all the clothes I wanted, I started in on my favorite knick-knacks and photographs, pictures of my dad and me before he died, several of my friends and me. Then, I went into the bathroom and raided my makeup case, almost forgetting my favorite scent—Jo Malone's Pomegranate Noir. I spritzed some on just for good measure.

Hefting the duffle onto my shoulder, glad for my increased strength, I went back into the living room, carefully skirting around the outline of the body. I stood there, tapping my lip trying to remember what it was I wanted in that room.

"How could I forget?" I said, with a snap of my fingers.

I hurried over to my desk and opened the middle drawer. With a grin of satisfaction, I drew out my mp3 player, all 80 gigabytes filled with my favorite music. Hours and hours of music. Days, even. Also in the drawer were the solar charger I used for camping and my ear buds. All went into the duffle.

Putting the bag down, I reached for one last item: my Boise sound system for the player.

Music was to be shared.

After ensuring all my items were safely stored, I zipped

up the duffle and looked around again at what was once my home.

"Bren?" I asked.

"Rose?" he replied, turning from my bookcase, where he and Joss had been browsing.

"What I would really like to do right now is draw a big, old smiley face in the middle of all that fingerprint chalk dust." I looked over to him. "Wouldn't that be a surprise for somebody to discover the thief who took Rose Malone's things was Rose Malone, herself?"

"It would also leave our enemies a message," he replied, hesitantly.

"Fuck yeah, it would!" I replied. I wiped my tears with the back of my fist, drew my smiley face and then proceeded to put as many of my finger and hand prints over the carefully dusted crime scene as possible. I hoped that news of this would somehow make it to Lacy. Of all my friends, I think she'd have taken my death the hardest, just because she was my editor. I'm sure she would feel it was somehow her fault. That's how she was.

When I was done I looked at Bren who had already slung my duffle over his shoulder, and stood waiting with Joss under his arm.

I smiled.

"Ready?" he asked.

"Yup," I said, looking around one last time. "I sure would like to be a fly on the wall when the detectives next come into this room."

I accepted Bren's outstretched hand.

———

We left the way we had come.

Chapter 24 - A Different Kind of Peace

Bren lit a fire while I cleaned up the dishes. The seasons were slipping towards autumn, with longer nights and a chill in the air. I liked that Montorea had seasons. But the change of season also reminded me time was passing.

I had noticed Bren had been going more frequently to Sal 5. I never asked about it, but I assumed it had something to do with the League. I never asked, because I appreciated the alone time it allotted me. Being separate from Bren allowed me to work on my two lists in privacy. I was happy to see how long the "Things I Know About Bren-the-Man" list was growing. And a little unnerved about what I was learning from the "Things I Feel when Bren and I Are Together vs. What my Corpus Feels" list.

I came back into the living room, wiping the excess water onto my pants, and sat on the couch to watch Bren coaxing the fire to life, its flickering light highlighting the blond in his curls. He had let his hair get even shaggier, and I liked that.

"Bren?"

"Hmmm?" he replied, still focused on his task. He reached for a midsized log and set it in place on top of the kindling, allowing plenty of space for air. He blew gently on the embers.

I shivered.

"What's happening with the League? Did they find out anything interesting from the mem-unit download I did? "

He cocked an eyebrow at me. "Your information was very helpful on several levels."

"Really? How so?"

"Linda recognized where you had been contained." He paused, turning away from the fire and searched my face, "She also recognized your interrogator."

I stiffened. It was still an unpleasant memory. But as the weeks went by, the more I adjusted to my new life, the less I felt like a victim. I simply was no longer that person. It would not happen again. I knew that at a gut level, and I felt strong and capable.

"So, now what?" I asked.

"This does not bother you? This conversation?" he asked.

I smiled. "Not at all." I told him. "In fact, I'm surprised at how little it bothers me. I felt a twinge when you spoke of my interrogator, but I'm no longer that person. Anyway, however much I've enjoyed this peaceful place, and the time I've been allowed to adjust," I shrugged again, "I feel like it's time to get more involved. I know I am ready, 'cuz I'm getting a little bored." I chuckled.

Bren sat back on his heels, running a hand through his

hair. "Why do you think you should be involved?"

I blinked. "Besides the fact you said I could when I was ready? Well, I would think it was obvious." I gestured towards him. "You and me, the connection we have, the Silistel corpus. And," I added, "After I saw what they did to my apartment, once I got over being mad, I thought about how much power those people must have to have faked a crime scene. That cannot be allowed to continue. It's just so wrong."

He smiled, his face shifting into the expression of someone very old trying to be patient with someone very young. I have always hated that expression when I'm on the receiving end. It meant I was going to be told something I did not want to hear.

"Rose," he began as I tried not to roll my eyes. "About that promise I made to you about participating? I'm afraid I was overruled."

"Overruled? But I thought you were the leader of the League."

"I am, but not when it comes to you," he said, patiently, "I was told your corpus and the League are two unrelated topics. You are...'" he paused, trying to find the right words, "...an incident. You are not part of the League, nor have you been trained as a PeaceKeeper."

"An *incident*?" I sputtered. "I beg to differ, Mr. I-Don't-Want-To-Be-the-Only-Silistel-Corpus-in-Existence!"

He held up his hand and sort of patted the air between us. "It was a weak moment. I wanted you safe. And yes, you are right—I was wrestling with the isolation of being different. I deeply regret my judgment and choice. My actions went against my principles." His shoulders slumped. "You should not have been subjected to this. We have other protocols that should have been followed. Your life would still have been spared..." his voice trailed off.

I cocked my head at him and squinted. "What other protocols?" I asked quietly. "What aren't you telling me?"

He glanced up and sighed, rising in one easy move to take a seat beside me. "If an innocent's life is in jeopardy, we have a protocol where we take the innocent, wipe clean their memory, and give them a life upon another planet. Their life is spared and the mission is also protected."

I looked down at my hands for several moments, listening to the popping and snap of the fire. I sighed. "Okay, well, for what it's worth, I am very glad that's not what happened to me."

"As am I," he said.

I glanced up, studying him. "You would truly have been alone," I said.

Bren nodded, his eyes showing nothing, but the connection between us speaking volumes.

"And they still could have found me," I pointed out.

"Although it would have been unlikely," he said. "You would have been protected."

"But this way I can protect myself. And..." I added, "You are protected as well."

Again he nodded.

"And now both you and I are invulnerable."

"Yes."

"Yes." I answered, and waited for him to continue, but he did not. "What, Bren? What aren't you telling me?"

He took a breath and looked skyward. "There is a great concern about what you are—a 3rd with an indestructible corpus. There is also a great concern about my judgment and position as a PeaceKeeper."

"Meaning?"

"Meaning, I may be banned from the Keepers by my actions. It is under consideration. If it weren't for Langsford's faith in me, I would have been banned already."

I shook my head. "That's ironic, you who have never needed the rehab." I touched his hand. "I am sorry, Bren."

He smiled softly. "I do not regret it."

I felt myself beginning to glow. "Nor do I."

We both sat glowing with an inner fire, enjoying the mere fact we were what we were and we were together.

"It was not just because I did not want to be the only Silistel corpus in existence, Rose," Bren said softly. "It was that the only other Silistel corpus in existence would be you."

He reached for me then, and I nearly surrendered to my feelings.

Nearly.

"I need to know something, Bren," I whispered, my palm on his chest. His heart was beating strong and sure beneath my palm. So steady. Just like the man.

He held still.

"Do you have great concern about what I am?" I could have easily gotten the answer through our connection, but I needed to hear him tell me.

Out loud.

We may both have Silistel corpuses, but I still saw myself as a 3rd and he as a 5th.

"Oh, my dear Rose," he replied, his body becoming more luminescent by the moment, "how can you even doubt?" He smiled so gently, so very sweetly. "You are my heart. You are my home."

This time I reached for him and discovered I, too, was home.

* * *

"Why do you withdraw from me, Rose?"

We were lying entwined in front of the fire on a pile of blankets we had hastily snatched from our beds. Our clothes were strewn around the room.

I propped myself up on my elbow to look at him.

Bren pushed my curls off my face, out of my eyes.

"What do you mean?"

He glanced at himself, then at us, our bodies warm and glowing. "This could be so much more."

I laughed. "More? That wasn't enough?"

"We could truly merge our minds and emotions." he caressed my face, his hand moving down to my shoulder. "But you have built a wall. I felt you holding back," he paused. "It could be more," he repeated.

I smiled and sighed, snuggling back down and curling around him. "I am sure it *will* be more." My voice sounded muffled. "But for now?" I thought back on our lovemaking.

The intensity. "For now, I just want to savor what was. It's nice to know it could be more Bren, but…" I shook my head and smiled into his side, "…that was the most amazing bit of love-making I've ever experienced, and I want to just be with that." I felt his arm hold me closer as he stroked my hair. I sighed again. "Bliss," I murmured, drowsy and satiated.

"Bliss," he agreed. "Why do you keep yourself separate from me, Rose? It feels wrong."

Why was this topic so important to him? And, at the moment, I didn't have a complete thought in my head, floating in the afterglow as I was.

"Mmmph," was all I had the energy for. I touched his face with my fingertips and sent to him just exactly what I was feeling.

"Rest well, my Rose." I heard the laughter in his voice as he spooned himself around me. A man pleased with his own virility.

* * *

"Why do you keep yourself separate from me Rose?" Bren asked for a third time as we sat side by side on the couch, feeding each other breakfast. I glanced at where we touched.

There was absolutely no space between us.

I laughed. "I'm not sure how much closer we could get," I answered, deliberately misunderstanding him.

He started to get that patient teacher expression of his, and I interrupted him, putting the bowl we were sharing onto the coffee table and maneuvering myself to face him. "Bren, I know what you are asking. I just wanted to put off this conversation a little longer. But…," I sighed, "…I can see you won't let me." I tucked my curls behind my ears and thought about how to explain my feelings to him. Of course, it would have been a whole lot easier if I just touched him and downloaded what I was feeling, but that would defeat my purpose. I wanted to use words.

"Tell me again why you have never evolved beyond being a 5th."

His eyes widened a little as the understanding hit him. "If I evolved," he replied, "I would forfeit being a PeaceKeeper." He reached out and stroked my knee where it bumped up against his thigh. "You want to keep separate so you remain a 3rd."

I nodded. "But it's a little more than that. It's for two reasons, really. The first is yes, I see myself as an Ambassador of Earth to those in command, here. I wish I could get more involved." I held up my hand, halting his interruption. "I know you were talking about some politics yesterday, questioning your behavior, and I want to understand more of that, but let me finish."

I paused, trying to find my place again, "Okay, reason number one is I am in a unique position to represent 3rd thinking and feelings. Reason number two is just as important, Bren. Perhaps more so."

I took a breath. "It's about us. When we….touch with the intention of sharing our knowledge…when you send me information or when I send you information, we are so merged I have trouble knowing where you leave off and where I begin. There are no boundaries. I feel as if I have no idea who I am anymore, and it frightens me. Remember my reaction with the plants a few weeks back?"

He nodded, his face as inscrutable and calm as a Buddha, what I'd learned is his I'm-listening-intently expression.

"Just like with the plants, Bren. It still feels like death to me."

I covered his hand with my own, sending my feelings and reminding him how I felt back on Salinio 5, right after I had relived his memory of Astragon 7 from a 5th frequency, and again, the memories from when we communicated with the plants. Immediately he understood. In turn, he sent me his feelings and understanding. Although he let me know he wasn't in agreement, I felt soothed.

I relaxed and fed him a little round fruit that burst with flavor when you bit into it, kind of like a grape.

"Rose?" Bren asked.

"Hmmmm?" I smiled at him, wanting to see his dimple.

I was disappointed.

"Have you noticed when we take turns sharing our information by touch there is no merging?" His blue eyes were serious as he scanned my face.

I straightened. "Oh, my God, you're right!" I exclaimed with a half a laugh. "It's more like a conversation and less like a merging." I paused, watching his dimple appear. "That works! I believe we've just discovered some mind merging etiquette!"

"Etiquette?" he asked, looking at me rather quizzically.

"A polite protocol. You know, taking turns and sharing information, each being aware of themselves and the other person. Such a difference. When we were playing hide and seek, when we were reaching to find each other…" I shuddered. "So invasive. Where was my privacy?"

"And where was mine?" he asked softly.

I glanced sharply at him. "I never thought of that," I told him. "What was that like for you?"

"Invasive, but I knew it was you." He flashed his dimple at me, continuing, "I had nanobots throughout my system, constantly reporting my statistics. With just a thought, I destroyed them. Why would I worry that my mind could be invaded without my consent?

I brightened. "And if you can do that, then so could I. Therefore, I, too, have nothing to worry about." I was silent, thinking about all of it. "Perhaps, as I practice, I will be able to merge with the plants and all life like a 9th can." I fed him another grape-like fruit. "But not today."

We shared a few more bites of food and then my leg started to fall asleep, so I scooted over to sit beside him, stretching my legs out in front of me. I started rubbing my leg as it began to tingle back to life. "Maybe if I merged with everything, my damned extremities would learn not to fall asleep," I muttered.

"Would you like to come to a meeting with me this afternoon?" Bren asked abruptly.

I stopped rubbing my leg to stare at him. "With the League?" I asked hopefully.

"The League will be there," he replied. "So too, the Division heads of the Keepers and the Watchers."

I gasped.

"What's on the agenda?" I asked cautiously.

"Just what you might expect," came his reply, "They

will be discussing your future. I feel they need to see you to understand you are no threat."

Chapter 25 - The League is Dead

When we arrived, they were all there: LeFlow who, to Bren, was all lovely and elegant, and to me was just kind of odd and creepy-looking; Tomal, who looked like a huge toad or giant bulldog (I was debating that one), and Major General Carringdon in all her blueness and perfect hairdo.

The blue Division head frowned when she saw me, but said nothing. I could tell she was taken aback and did not like surprises.

"And here is your opportunity to be Earth's ambassador," Bren whispered to me, making me glad I took my time selecting what to wear. I'd picked a simple dress (made in America), nothing fancy, that made me feel feminine yet strong.

The League stood until asked to sit. The meeting began without preamble.

"We are preparing an ARK for Earth," Carringdon stated, "and we are dissolving the League." She held up her hand when Bren started to speak. "You will have an opportunity to voice your opinions, Captain, in a moment. We are not comfortable with this latest turn of events," she explained, looking directly at me. I was glad for all my martial arts training when her gaze shifted from mine first.

I glanced at Bren. His expression was closed, his mouth set in a grim line. I glanced at the others. Clearly they were just as unhappy with this news.

Bren cleared his throat.

Again Carringdon held up her hand. "There is more," she said, her gaze including us all. "With great gratitude to each of you for your hard work, we have learned enough and have taken measures to contain the sources of sabotage. Those who volunteered for the seed atom experiments during that phase of the Silistel Corpus Project have been relieved of their duties and are on extended leaves of absence until an undetermined date." She looked at Frankie and Mac saying, "I am sorry, but you two will be relieved as well."

I glanced at them. Mac seemed deflated, although his expression was blank, eyes straight ahead. Frankie looked back at me with a small, sad smile. It suddenly occurred to me these were two individuals who had committed their lives to be PeaceKeepers. And now they were in a very similar situation as I—suddenly expected to carve out a new way of being, a new identity. In this instance, misery did not like company.

Carringdon smiled softly at Bren. "The Corps has greatly benefitted from your being a part of it, Captain," she began. "We are all very much aware of your fine attributes and your many successes."

She paused, folding her hands together on the tabletop.

Here it comes, I thought and reached for Bren's hand

under that same table.

"So it is with gratitude and sorrow we are discharging you from your duties, Captain Faulkner. You will receive the highest honors available, and you will be well taken care of for the rest of your days. We truly wish the best for you, and we hope you will now allow yourself to continue your evolution."

The room exploded into sound, everyone speaking at once.

My senses reeled from the blasts of emotions. Yet, through our connection, I felt only calm emanating from Bren. I glanced at him and he smiled at me and shrugged, sending me images and feelings of the two of us and of freedom.

I smiled back and shrugged, too, showing him an image of Astragon 7.

But I sensed there was something he was not sharing with me....yet.

When the chaos subsided, LeFlow turned her large eyes toward me.

They were scary large. Alien large.

She reached out and touched me, then shuddered.

So did I.

"We have a great concern over the capabilities of Rose Malone," the Watcher told the group, looking directly at Bren. "Would she be willing to have her mind wiped?" she asked as if I were absent from the room.

I bristled, but Bren sent me a thought message. *I believe they wish to test your reaction. Stay calm, my love.*

Understood, I thought back.

It was Mac who came to my defense.

"By the balls of all male sentients!" he exploded, "I cannot sit here and say nothing!" He pointed at me. "That girl is an angel. She would never hurt a single sentient. Ever." He said and sat back, arms folded, glowering at LeFlow. My knight.

"I will hold responsibility for her," Ian said before anyone could respond to Mac's outburst. "I am still a part of the Corps, and I will hold responsibility."

"Ian," Bren began.

"Hush, Bren," Ian told him softly. "She is family," he said, smiling at me.

I swallowed, looking at Ian through a haze of tears.

"Accepted," Carringdon said before Bren could argue further.

There was one final announcement.

When order was restored, Major General Fins Langsford officially stepped down from his position as head of the Guardians.

The meeting adjourned.

What was going to happen to Earth?

I hadn't even had the chance to practice my Ambassador skills.

Chapter 26 - Long Live the League

The cabin seemed the most natural place for us to gather after such an uproar, and it was where Bren took the League.

Its peaceful setting was the direct opposite of a sterile construct orbiting around a planet belching out soldiers and giant spaceships. I sighed, realizing I really was a Planet-Strider.

Wordlessly Bren led us into the kitchen, where we found ourselves sitting around the kitchen table. Mac dragged over a chair from the desk in the front room. Langsford sat on a stool, his knees nearly at the level of his chin. Ian opted for the kitchen countertop. Frankie and I sat in the two remaining chairs. It seemed ironic, just a few minutes ago, we had been sitting around a high-tech meeting table. I picked at one of the table's grommets.

Bren had remained standing so he could pace. "Does anyone wish to comment?" he asked, pausing in his pacing.

"Apparently the League is no longer required," Ian said, smiling slightly. "It was very dramatic for the dissolution of a group."

I crossed my arms and took a deep breath. "So what is the normal protocol?"

"Generally, people are simply reassigned," Mac told me, bleakly. "By the balls, I never thought this day would be upon me."

Frankie nodded sadly. "What is to be done with us?"

Langsford stretched out one leg and adjusted his seating. "Memory-wipe most likely," he commented softly, "for the two of you."

Frankie gasped.

Mac went white.

"And for the rest of us?" asked Ian.

"I would think we would be rehabbed," Bren said.

Langsford nodded.

"But nobody has been misaligned," I pointed out. "You were all following your orders."

"To ensure the integrity of the Corps, it is what I would recommend," said Langsford. "The League found openings for sabotage. And these final steps will close those openings."

Bren leaned against the kitchen counter by his brother. "Did you volunteer to step down?" he asked Langsford.

Langsford shook his head. "Yes and no," he answered. "It was recommended I do so, and I would have recommended the same."

"And who will be replacing you?" asked Ian.

"Renaut Neeradyne," Langsford said, a name I had

never heard, even from Bren's mem-unit.

"Who is she?" asked Bren, shaking his head.

"Head of the Guardians' secret organization," Ian chimed in.

Langsford looked sharply at Ian, who shrugged, "It's my job find out about things," he said.

"And you are very good at it," Langsford replied.

Ian nodded. "That I am."

"I do not want my mind wiped," Frankie said. Her sorrow was palpable.

Mac rubbed his face. "Nor I," he replied. "All those expletives," he said, shaking his head woefully, "gone."

I nodded. Poor Mac, I thought to myself, his one passion taken from him in a matter of seconds, solely to contain the integrity of the PeaceKeepers.

It started to dawn on me these so-called more advanced 5ths and 7ths were still very much like 3rds in many respects. I tabled the thought, but I promised myself to think about it when I had the chance. It felt like something important, something that had been overlooked for a long, long time.

"There are always choices," stated Bren.

Mac glanced at him hopefully.

"Suppose we continue the League of Five?"

Frankie's eyes widened. "Against orders?" she gasped.

"Suppose we did?" Bren asked.

"Why?" asked Langsford, "We found the source of the saboteurs. We've plugged the holes. Mission accomplished."

"And an ARK is being readied," Bren replied, "Which means the Scouts will begin to move, and there is still not enough known about what is actually taking place on that planet."

"Finally!" I exclaimed.

Langsford waved his hand, "That planet has been monitored for thousands of years," he said dismissively, "I think we know enough."

"Yet they managed to sabotage several of our missions without leaving their home planet," Ian said softly, adding, "and we have just learned about this," he held up a finger to stop Langsford's retort. "What I find most interesting is, if my brother had not been given his Silistel corpus with its abilities to detect subtleties within shifts of energy, we would still not know."

He leaned forward, "Smyke was pegged for advancement. He was being groomed for Division head," he said, holding Langsford's gaze. "Can you imagine a scenario where a Division head was being handled by a group of paranoid 3rds?"

Bren chuckled at Langsford's expression, breaking the tension mounting in the room. "My brother makes a very good point," he said. "I propose we take the League to Earth and see what we can uncover from there."

He looked at us all, his gaze including me. "Who would be better equipped for such a scouting mission?" He smiled at me, and I saw his dimple, "We even have a citizen of that planet to help us blend in more fully."

"A fine idea," Langsford said slowly, "but unfortunately, I am unable to request the documentation we would require. It would make it impossible for us to go there with identities. And, given the climate of Earth, I for one, would want to have perfect copies of identification."

"Impossible for you, perhaps," said Bren, "but not for Code Breaker."

He nudged his brother who grinned.

I swore I heard Ian begin to salivate.

Ian looked at me, "What would they say on Earth?" he asked with a wink, "A piece of cake?"

Chapter 27 - Earthward Ho!

Getting ready for a Scouting Mission reminded me of planning a camping trip into the wilderness. One had to think of everything that could possibly go wrong so one could be as prepared as possible.

That's where I came in.

Bren had assigned Ian and me to be the List Masters. We created the lists of the necessities and then Bren, Mac and Frankie collected everything.

We decided the cabin would be our headquarters. I moved my things into Bren's room, while the others turned my room into a receiving area Frankie had organized into different categories. (All overseen by my cardboard model of Joss Walker, I might add. Despite, or rather, because of, Bren's annoyance, Joss had managed to find his way into my bedroom after all.) The desk was used for the necessary documentation. The bed was used for our clothing, all neatly stacked with our names on them. One corner was used for the technical gear the Keepers used for scanning, communicating and monitoring. Another corner was for medical equipment.

Since they were no longer on duty, Mac and Frankie stayed with Ian. It made it easier for Bren or me to teleport them back and forth if they were all in one place. How I envied their beds and baths!

There had been a big discussion about weapons. I argued against them, even though I was told they would only be used for self-protection. It just didn't feel right to me, PeaceKeepers coming to Earth carrying weapons. I knew I'd never use them. But I also understood protecting oneself. After all, I had years of martial arts training underneath my black belt.

"I had thought an advanced race would be beyond weapons," I told them. "It's a little disappointing."

"Do you not carry any defensive weaponry against wild animals when you enter their natural habitat?" Langsford asked. "If this were a normal scouting mission, the Guardians would handle the weaponry, but we are acting outside of the Corps, now, and must do what is necessary."

He had a point. I took pepper spray with me when hiking in grizzly country. Earth might be my natural habitat, but it was not theirs.

Working outside of the Corps made acquiring all of our supplies more difficult. When we could, we purchased supplies from the neighboring towns. But the necessary Corps equipment could only be gotten from the Corps.

Bren solved the problem.

He had Ian Code Breaker find a variety of locations where the equipment could be acquired. Then, he would teleport to the different places, bringing back the items, never taking more than one or two of the same thing from the same place. That way, missing items would be chalked up as inventory glitches. I think Bren enjoyed hopping from place to place and honing his skills. He went to a ship for one item, an ARK stationed who-knows-where for another. He even helped himself to a supply transport carrier while it was in InnerSpace. He was very proud of that particular trip. It was quite an impressive feat.

After that trick, I decided I really needed to practice more as well. As it turned out, as soon as Ian created our fake identification, I had plenty of time to practice.

Both Bren and I went together to Earth to pick the best place to settle. Since we could teleport, and bring others with us, it was decided the best way to hide would be where we would least be expected. Cities were usually the best places to hide, but then privacy was dicey.

"So what we need is a place where people come and go, but no one really knows anyone, and there is privacy, right?" I asked Bren, working out a solution.

"That would be ideal," he answered.

"Come with me," I told him as I reached for his hand.

I took him to Kona, on the Big Island of Hawaii.

"What do you think?" I asked, inhaling the sweet scent of Plumeria. "It's a prime destination for honeymooners," I told him, as I fitted myself into his embrace. "No one will notice a thing," I said as I nuzzled his neck.

"Brilliant," Bren replied. "Let's tell the others." He tightened his embrace. "In a minute."

I sighed into his kiss.

One of my concerns was language, but the Corps had

that covered with microscopic language chips Bren had Doc Gauge implant directly into everyone's brains.

"Do you already have a chip implant?" I asked Bren when he had told Doc the number of chips he'd need. I was invited to watch, but I declined. Hearing about the procedure was enough, although Frankie assured me it didn't hurt.

"I've noticed I no longer have language issues," he answered. "I believe it's the corpus."

"Interesting," I replied. "I thought the reason I had no trouble understanding people was because of my mem-unit experience when I first got here. I guess there's more to learn about myself."

On the very day Montorea experienced its first frost of the season, we teleported ourselves to Hawaii.

We stood in a semicircle in the doorway of my old bedroom, gazing at everything we had assembled. It appeared all was in readiness for our departure. We buttoned down the cabin, not knowing how many Earth days we might be away, then stood together in a circle, holding our gear in our hands.

Bren looked at each of us.

"Ready?" he asked.

"Are we bringing the cardboard man, then?" Mac asked. "For luck?"

Frankie giggled and nudged Mac.

"I think not," Bren said dryly.

"He can guard the place while we're gone, Mac," I told him, keeping my expression serious.

Ian coughed and glanced at me with a wink.

Bren cleared his throat. "Are we ready?" he asked again.

There was a low murmur of assent.

He looked at me and nodded.

Together, we merged our minds and focused on teleporting the League and all our stuff to the Big Island of Hawaii.

Chapter 28 - Planet-Striders

I was sitting at a long collapsible table, scrolling through social networking sites, not really sure what we were looking for, but jotting down things that stood out to me. If I understood Ian correctly, a pattern usually formed, and a reading of the general mood of the communicating globe could be taken.

Beside me were six other laptops, their little engines whirring along, sorting through pixels and bytes of data in accordance with six different algorithms Ian had programmed. They seemed much more efficient than I, but Ian had assured me what I was doing—perusing the social networks—was just as important.

"You are our gateway into the mind of Earth's sentients," he told me. "I could easily overlook something because I considered it moot."

Ian had a way of making one feel important. I bet his kids fought over who got to take out the trash.

Ian sat across from me, his face lit up by his own laptop screen as he studied the migratory patterns of whales and dolphins, Earth's other sentients. His side of the table looked identical to mine, with six laptops running six different algorithms.

I sighed and rubbed my eyes, then stretched the kink out of my back.

Ian glanced up at me. "Want a break?"

I looked at the digital clock on my laptop and shook my head with a smile. "Frankie and Mac should be here, soon. I'll take a break then."

He nodded absently, already deep into his work once more.

I had to admit I was a little uneasy about Frankie and Mac. It was their first solo trip to the shopping area in Kona. I felt like a mother waiting for their teen to come home from their first prom, hoping they had a good time, but wanting them safely back.

I glanced at the time again. They actually weren't too late, not late enough to worry about, and I refocused on my Twitter stream.

The sound of a screen door opening interrupted my focus. It was followed by the aroma of sweet Plumeria, fresh Hibiscus, and a blast of moist, salty heat as Mac, arms burdened with a box, held the door open with his foot, allowing Frankie to slip past him carrying an equally large box she could barely see over.

"I don't remember the shopping list being that sizable," I commented.

"Holy Crap of the Mother Goddess!" exclaimed Mac happily. "Rarely have I seen so many interesting items for purchase in one area. Look at these!" he said holding up a boxed set of the Chronicles of Joss Walker, Emissary of Evolution.

"You've got to be kidding me!" I exclaimed.

Mac lifted an eyebrow, "I thought it would make nice, light reading to pass the time."

"Hey!" exclaimed Frankie. "You're not keeping those for yourself. You have to share."

"You squabble like my boys," chuckled Ian. "We will all read them together. Since I have the best speaking voice, I will do the reading. They can be our evening entertainment for the duration of this mission."

Frankie cheered.

I groaned.

"Now if only we'd brought the cardboard man," Mac mused.

Ian and I got up, stretched and followed the parade into the kitchen.

Putting the boxes on the counter, Mac withdrew a couple of foam noodles. "Flotation devices," he told Ian, waiving them around like large antennae.

"Think fast, Rose!" said Frankie, proud of her slang, although her accent still needed a lot of work. She threw me a pair of bright green board shorts, holding up a second pair to herself.

"Thanks," I told her, "We'll fit right in with the rest of the tourists."

"This is a lovely land," she said. "My home planet is mostly land and lakes. It is one massive continent. But here," she swept her hand, taking in the island, "the wind is sultry, yet fresh. This land is like a large open ARK floating on a vast blue ocean."

"You would call that an 'island,'" Ian commented dryly.

I giggled, swept up in Frankie's enthusiasm.

* * *

Since I had cooking duty, I fixed our dinner—a lovely mahi-mahi caught fresh that morning—which we'd enjoyed together around the dining room table. I was happy it turned out so well, as I had been experimenting with steaming them in parchment with mango salsa.

I looked at my companions, marveling, only a few months ago, I hadn't known they existed. It hit me then how settled I was in my new life. I shot a glance at Bren and sent him a whisper of energy. Though deep in conversation with his brother, I felt an answering warmth wend its way through my person.

I sighed happily, finally knowing to my core Bren the Man, unfiltered, was so much better than the filtered Bren who was the character Joss Walker. Damn, I wished Lacy could have met him. It was so tempting, now I was back on Earth, to get a message to Lacy. Of course, I wouldn't, and it made me sad she thought, as everybody else, a crazed fan had killed me. Because of it, my books were selling like hotcakes. There was even talk of making an Emissaries of Evolution movie. Too bad I couldn't collect postmortem royalty checks.

Mac stood and took my plate along with his own back to the kitchen. Soon I heard water running as he began cleaning up the mess I had made.

"That was very good, Rose, I thank you," Langsford said, carefully wiping his mustache with a napkin. Of all of us, I had noticed the biggest change with him. He had softened, let his guard down, and didn't feel as rigid to me. His voice was not as clipped, either.

I rested my forearms on the table and leaned towards him, "Have you been on many scouting missions?" I asked.

He shook his head, "It has been many years, and none like this."

"Do you feel a little lost," I asked, "you know, since you no longer are a Division head?"

He shrugged, smoothing out his napkin with both hands. "It was an unexpected occurrence and one not of my choosing," he replied guardedly. "Never in the history of the Guardians has such an event transpired. I have a deep regret," he glanced at Frankie as she rose to clear the table and help Mac. His expression softened, "And I have more freedom as well." he added looking back at me. "And adjustments."

I nodded with a small smile and glanced at Frankie's slight form disappearing into the kitchen.

"Not all adjustments are unpleasant," he said, following my gaze.

I winked at him, mouthing the words "Congratulations," and then I stifled a giggle. "Did I just make the inscrutable Fins Langsford blush?" I whispered at him.

His shade went a deeper red while he pretended he hadn't heard me.

I glanced at Bren and Ian. They were in an animated argument that had been ongoing since boyhood. I decided it would never be resolved. They were having too much fun arguing over it.

I leaned back, extending my senses as I extended my legs, and closed my eyes as I surreptitiously scanned the group. Bren and I often did that to get a sense of the others.

From each of my new comrades I felt a sense of companionship and belonging, myself included.

It was a nice feeling, I decided.

Mac came in flicking dishwater from his fingers and sat down.

Frankie followed with a box of chocolate-covered macadamia nuts and a plate of sliced papaya.

Mac cleared his throat. "Bren, have you thought about Linda's request?" he asked. "She has asked me again."

A couple of days ago Linda had asked to meet with us, which had taken all of us by surprise. Not only was it against protocol, but also several weeks before she had told us all handlers were being reinstated to other departments. Apparently when the leaks had been plugged on the PeaceKeepers' end, the ripple effect had shut down a whole department here on Earth. Essentially blind, the PeaceKeepers' antagonists could no longer move forward with their plan to infiltrate and destroy from within. It was back to the drawing board for them.

In the meantime, they were all going silent and taking cover. Since they were aware of the Keepers' MO, they knew an ARK would be sent to infiltrate and support Earth's Awakening process. They knew it would take thirty to fifty years to arrive, and that wasn't much time for them to prepare a defense against the ARK's arrival.

My poor planet!

So riddled with fear.

Mac had been devastated. Anyone with a pinch of sensitivity could see he had fallen in love with Linda.

And Linda? Was she just as devastated? I had only my impressions from Bren's mem-unit. From my experience, I knew how close one could become from sharing thoughts, from being within one another's minds. I did not doubt how swiftly love could grow.

So when Linda, after weeks of silence, had contacted Mac for a rendezvous, he was elated. And crestfallen when Bren was not equally elated, especially when he had learned Mac had told Linda our group was coming to Earth.

"You would jeopardize the success of our mission for this woman?" His voice had been like flint. "We may no longer be a part of the Corps, Mac, but we still follow a chain of command and time-tested protocols."

Bren had asked Mac to allow Linda to speak with him directly. When she took over Mac's body, Bren had felt a difference.

"There is something not right with the overlay," he had told me privately. "I no longer trust Linda."

"Then don't, Bren," I had replied. "You would know," adding, "and we Earthlings are a paranoid and frightened bunch."

So Bren told Mac no meeting would be arranged, "It could be a trap, Mac," he had explained. "We will not risk it."

Sorrowfully, Mac had relayed the news to Linda. When she heard, she panicked. She asked to speak with Bren in private and he agreed.

"She pleaded with me, Rose," he told me. "She feared for her life and had a good case." He paused. "Yet my Inner Knowing does not trust her truth."

"So what are you going to do?" I asked, seeing how torn he was.

I could understand his dilemma. If he was wrong and Linda was killed, both he and Mac would be devastated. Despite the part she played in this mess, Bren still considered her an innocent, and innocents were protected at any cost.

He had sighed and closed his eyes, soaking up the loving energy I had been sending him. "I will think on it, weigh my choices, and then decide," he had told me.

Bren sighed the same kind of sigh now as he studied Mac. "I am still against this rendezvous." He held up his hand to silence Mac's protest. "However, Langsford feels it would be wise to take the risk in order to acquire information."

"It is our purpose for being here," Ian agreed.

Langsford nodded.

"And so I decided Mac and I will go meet with Linda."

If Mac were able to glow like Bren and I, he would have.

I touched Bren's hand. "I'm going with you."

He shook his head. "If anything were to happen to me, you would be the team's only way home."

"How could anything happen to either of us?" I asked him. "We're indestructible."

"She has a point," said Ian.

I glanced at Ian with a smile of gratitude. "And I need

the training," I added. "I'd like to do something more than scan Twitter Tweets all day." I touched his hand again. "Please? I want to learn."

I want you safe, he told me silently, showing me how precious I was to him.

But I am safe. My corpus makes me safe. You make me safe, I silently replied, sending him love and showing him how powerful I felt.

Bren sighed and rubbed the back of his neck. "Very well. This will also be Rose's first training mission."

"My first mission!" I squealed, clasping my hands together.

Frankie laughed, clapping, while Langsford rolled his eyes.

Chapter 29 - Mac Buys the Farm, Again

Before we teleported to the rendezvous point, Bren went over our instructions one last time. "If anything is amiss," he said pointedly to me, "you are to take Mac and return here."

I nodded.

"Immediately," he said.

I nodded again.

"And no arguments."

"No arguments," I assured him. "You're the pro, here, Bren. I will follow your lead."

Satisfied, he turned to Mac. "And you," he said. "Keep your shield up at all times."

Mac nodded.

"Under no circumstances will you drop your shield. That is an order."

"Yes, sir," Mac replied.

We joined hands.

"Ready?" he asked.

At our nods, Bren teleported us to the coordinates Linda had provided.

We found ourselves in an underground parking garage, sparsely lit and gloomy. It smelled of old exhaust and oil, and was cold and damp.

A very far cry from the tropics.

I shivered.

We stood quietly as we adjusted our vision to the gloom. To my right I heard a gasp and the whisper of a footfall. I turned and saw Linda.

She was alone.

With a soft cry she raced toward us, an expression of joy on her face, her arms opened wide.

Bren put an arm out to hold Mac back, but he was too late.

With an answering shout of welcome, Mac surged forward to greet her, intent only on Linda's smiling, welcoming face.

And as he raced forward, oblivious to our warning shouts, Mac did exactly what Bren had told him not to do.

Mac dropped his shield.

He turned the thing completely off. Then, he opened his arms just as wide, waiting to envelop Linda in his embrace.

Linda rushed into his arms.

The blissful union instantly turned into a nightmare. Linda began hacking at Mac's neck with the box cutter she had secreted up her coat sleeve.

Too stunned to properly react, Bren and I watched as she sliced and tore, severing Mac's windpipe and cutting into arteries.

Blood sprayed everywhere—on Linda, on the ground—and poured down Mac's front.

I gagged.

With a howl, Linda threw the cutter as far away as possible and fled even before the cry stopped echoing off the walls of the empty garage.

Mac sank slowly to the cement floor.

"She's getting away!" I shouted, glancing at Bren as I started to take off after Linda.

But I froze at what I saw.

Having rushed to his side, Bren had kneeled down to gather Mac in his arms. He was staring down at his friend, mouth agape, with a look of stunned disbelief.

Meanwhile, Mac was making terrible gagging noises. His blood flowed freely in rhythmic spurts.

"Bren!" I shouted, banking down my own need to gag as the sight and smell of all that spurting blood filled my senses.

But Bren was frozen, his eyes riveted on his dying friend.

Frantic, I rushed to him and shook his shoulder, forcing him to look at me. "Bren! There's still time! Take him to Doc!"

He looked at me, his eyes flickering with recognition. "Rose," he said. "She slit his throat, Rose." His brow wrinkled with confusion and pain.

"Take him to Doc. *Now!*" I ordered. "We can figure all this out later."

I was mystified at Bren's reaction. He had felt something was off. We were prepared for trouble, except for one very important exception: a Resus scope. They are monitored so strictly we felt it was safer to just count on Bren's and my teleportation abilities.

"No!" He stated. "I am not leaving you, Rose."

"Yes. You. Will." I answered just as emphatically. "I can look after myself. I'm like you. I'll be okay."

"We don't know that!" he said, shaking his head. "I don't understand..."

Mac began to gasp louder, his eyes wide with fright. I could see the life flickering out, only a tiny thread remaining.

Anger flared through me. "Go, Bren! I will never forgive you if you don't save Mac." I told him through clenched teeth, shaking him.

"There's no time."

I punched him in the shoulder. Hard. "Then *make* the time, dammit! GO!"

He looked at me, still in shock.

"By the Flickering Balls of a Gurt, GO!" I shouted again.

He went.

In one instant he was there with Mac in his arms. In another, they were gone. Hearing one of Mac's expletives must have broken through Bren's shock.

All that remained was Mac's blood, clotted and thick. My stomach heaved again, but I shut off the reaction.

Scrambling to my feet, I took off after Linda, baffled by Bren's reaction.

Bren was the man of action, the man with all the answers. Yet he had frozen.

Knowing Bren, he was going to be extremely unhappy with himself and would not rest until he understood why he had frozen as he did. I would not rest, either, and I felt my own theories starting to coalesce.

First priority, however, was Linda.

As I ran, I felt my warrior mind, as I called it, begin to awaken, and I expanded and sharpened my senses.

I knew I looked petite, girly and helpless; a sweet little angel living in her fantasies.

But I'm not, although I consider my image my best defense.

In reality, the years of martial arts training, both physical and mental, have made me quite tough. And now, with my corpus, I'm a heck of a lot tougher.

Bad guys beware. As Mac would say, I was as pissed as Wereplevore in heat.

Chapter 30 - What about Linda?

I stopped worrying about Mac. I stopped worrying about Bren.

I became a hunter, focused only on my target.

I had to agree with Bren—something felt off about the whole episode.

I'd never met Linda, but I liked what I'd seen of her via Bren's experiences. Deep down I knew Linda wasn't a bad person...but a terrified, paranoid and the-aliens-are-invading type person?

Perhaps.

What alerted me to things being off wasn't anything Bren had felt. What alerted me was that horrible box cutter. If I were going to slit someone's throat, I would not use a box cutter. It's not what a woman would use to do the deed, because it's just not a practical weapon. A scalpel? Yes. But a box cutter? Definitely no. Way too messy.

I ran lightly and effortlessly, following Linda's fading footsteps with my heightened senses.

I was getting little red flags of emotions, as if my destination was not a good place. I also had a strange feeling of déjà vu. Could this be where I had been taken after my abduction? I was beginning to catch the first whiffs of disinfectant and my memories perked up. But my surroundings were darker than my memories. Maybe the same place but on a different floor?

I came to a T intersection. Just by chance, I glanced left before I glanced right, catching the last bit of movement as a door closed in the darkened hallway. I decided to proceed with caution. Either Linda was very stupid or I was being led into a trap. If I had just committed a murder, I would not take off running, just to hide in a room down the hall. I would most definitely get as far away from the murder site as possible.

Slowing to a soft walk, I took a deep breath and let it out softly as I crept closer to the door that had just closed. Reaching it, I paused and listened. The only sounds were coming from within that room. I could hear at least four different voices, none of them Linda's. They were all male. Tuning up my hearing, I started to make out what they were saying.

The assholes were congratulating each other!

"That worked perfectly," someone said.

"Got it all on video," said another.

"Think we can find their weak spot?" asked a third.

"Given time, I am certain of it," answered the first voice.

"You all know Linda was followed," said a slightly familiar voice. "Best get prepared for plan B."

And that was my cue.

I've gotta say it now, there's a certain amount of bravado that comes with knowing one is indestructible. And since it was my time to shine, I decided upon the Avenging Angel approach. I slammed opened the door with my mind and turned up the glow. But when I glanced over and saw Linda huddled and ignored off to the side, I stopped playing at Avenging Angel.

I became Avenging Angel.

The room was bright and I adjusted my eyes as I scanned the area, noting each individual's position in the room. In the corner I saw a flotation tank and the bells and whistles used to maintain it, along with recording equipment and a bank of monitors of all the corridors.

Note to self, in the future, to not believe empty corridors were harmless. Remember to scan for cameras. But since I was new at this PeaceKeeper business, I quickly forgave myself.

Two silent guards pointing large semi-automatic rifles stood between the four men and me who looked like they had just had some really good sex. Upon hearing my grand entrance, the four paused in the middle of helping a fifth man out of the floatation tank.

"You're handling Linda," I said, rather indignantly.

"Excellent observational skills," replied the man owning the slightly familiar voice. "Welcome to the party, Miss Malone. You're looking no worse for wear. Dare I say you are positively glowing?" he smirked.

The others smirked as well.

I really do not like smirkers.

A major deal-breaker.

I am a writer, and I do not believe I think as well on my feet as I do in front of a keyboard.

Having said that, I'm am still darn proud of what I did next.

I rushed over to Linda, who looked completely shattered, and gathered her in my arms, where she collapsed into wrenching sobs. She had never met me, but she was clinging to me like a lifeline, that's how distraught she was.

I poured love into her.

Simultaneously, I let my temper loose. This group of smirkers! They reminded me of grade school bullies who thought they had the upper hand.

Time to turn the tables.

I glanced about the room and saw just what I needed. Clipboards. Four of them. Good.

I mentally instructed the clipboards to begin thwacking the backsides of the four men.

Oh, but before they could get spanked, I mentally yanked all their pants and underwear down around their ankles as the clipboards remained stationary in mid-air until I forced them to bend over, their manhoods shriveling in the cold.

Not forgetting about the guards, I also pulled down their pants. Having their pants and undies yanked down by invisible hands distracted them from even attempting to shoot at me, which wouldn't have worked anyway, since I'd jammed the trigger mechanisms on their fancy guns.

In addition, I psychically shouted into the mind of

Linda's handler to never, EVER, *EVER* handle another person again, *EVER*, and I made him slap his own face—hard—each time I shouted the word EVER in his mind.

That last part I'm not as proud of, because I think I left some lasting psychological damage, although that jerk-of-a-handler deserved it.

Out loud I said to the smirkers, all the while glowing even brighter and radiating my anger towards them, "You are very naughty boys, and very naughty boys deserve a good spanking."

Then, I let them have it with the clipboards.

By their indignant and painful yelps, I knew they would remember my visit for a long, long while.

But, just in case, I had turned on their video recording equipment the minute I'd slammed open the door, so they could replay it at their leisure.

How was that for multi-tasking?

With Linda securely in my arms, I thought, *Clean, empty room. Waldorf Astoria. New York City.*

The next instant we were there.

I had always wanted to stay at the Waldorf.

Chapter 31 - At the Waldorf

We found ourselves in a room with warm, butter-yellow walls, a green patterned carpet and dark pink patterned sofa and chairs.

I gently helped Linda, still in a rather comatose state, to sit on a lovely French provincial chair of dark wood and dark rose velveteen that faced a cozy fireplace. Its high back cradled her body, offering a sense of security. I crossed over to the window to see the timeless beauty of the Chrysler Building filling the view. By closing the lovely gold and patterned drapes, I created a quiet little sanctuary of elegance and safety, so different from the cement room where we had just been.

I eyed Linda, still splattered with Mac's blood, its odor tainting the room.

"Let's get you cleaned up, shall we?" I spoke gently, as if to a frightened child. "I'll be right back, Linda." I touched her shoulder and sent her a feeling of safety and love.

The bathroom, with its black and white tiled floor, offered plenty of soft towels. I grabbed a couple and moistened a washcloth. Linda really needed a shower, but at least I could get the blood off her face and hands. On my way back to her, I grabbed a robe from the closet. The robe was plush and white, making me realize just how pale Linda was, since she nearly matched its color.

I continuously talked to Linda, just unimportant things, trying to be as soothing as possible, while I helped her clean up. Then I stripped her down to her underwear and bundled her into the robe. As I worked, she began to take note of her surroundings and of me.

"I should know you," she said, as if waking from a dream.

I nodded. "I am Rose Malone and you are Linda Carmichael."

"Rose! In the flesh! Oh, my God!" She looked around. "Where are we? Where are the others?"

"We're at the Waldorf Astoria." I told her. "What can you remember?"

"The Waldorf! But that's in New York! We should be in DC! How did I get here?"

"I brought you here," I grasped her hands. "Linda. Please focus for me. How much can you remember of the last few hours?"

She looked at me, puzzled. "Uh, well, the last I remembered was I was finally going to meet Mac," she blushed a little, "and you and Captain Faulkner. But..." her brow furrowed, "...what happened? That's all I can remember, other than a sick feeling that I did something horrible."

I sent soothing energy into her. "You were being handled, Linda," I said softly.

"What? How?" She shook her head. "That shouldn't be possible."

I shrugged. "Nonetheless, you were." I took a breath. "And we found out the hard way." I briefly told her what had happened and how I'd gotten her to where we were.

"Oh, God," she moaned, pulling her hands from my grip and burying her face in them. She shook her head as if to shake the truth from it. "Not Mac, please not Mac!" she cried.

"Hush Linda," I said gently, stroking her hair. "Bren is with Mac. There was time. It will be fine."

I hoped I was right.

I looked around and saw a carafe of chilled white wine on a side table with two clean glasses, as if waiting for us. I filled one of the glasses, thinking we should probably leave for Hawaii. Obviously the wine was waiting for somebody else. I sighed, looking at the elegant room, and amended my decision. I would find another unoccupied room for us.

I encouraged Linda to drink the wine. She nearly drained the glass.

"Since there was wine here, Linda, I think we should find ourselves another room." I poured her some more wine. "You sit tight while I tidy up, and then we'll go." She nodded calmly, impressing me with how well she was adjusting to all of this strangeness. Then I realized she'd actually had more exposure to all the space alien stuff than I had.

Pulling a pillowcase off of a spare pillow I found in the closet, I jammed it full of the towels, washcloth and Linda's bloody clothing. I looked around. Other than a few missing towels and one robe, the room looked ready for a guest.

I turned to Linda, who looked much more relaxed now

that she'd drunk half a carafe of the wine. "Are you ready to find another room?"

She nodded, eyes a tad unfocused.

"Take my hand, then," I instructed.

She rose and reached for my hand. I grasped it tightly within my own. I began to think about where to go next, but then paused. Glancing at Linda, I winked, "On second thought..." I told her, "...we can't let a good wine go to waste."

I tucked the towel-filled pillowcase under my arm, freeing my hand so that I could grab the carafe and the other glass, which I handed to Linda, making sure she had a good grip on our refreshments.

"Now!" I told her, taking her free hand.

The next room was smaller. It had the same buttery walls, but the carpet was a pale blue grey and the two plush chairs, more like mini-couches, were a solid yellow.

It came with an honor bar and snacks.

* * *

Linda was emotionally exhausted. After a long shower, she had curled up in a glorious king bed with crisp white linens. With a yawn and a sigh, she was soon asleep.

That's one way of dealing with a shock, I thought, watching her relax into the deep, rhythmic breaths of a dreamless sleep.

I softly closed the door and returned to the adjoining room. (If I was going to stay at the Waldorf for free, I might as well have my own room, too.) I reached my mind out for Bren.

He was at my side in an instant, looking relieved to see

me. With a touch, he let me know Mac was alive. With a touch, I caught him up on my side of the story. His eyebrows shot up when he saw what I'd done to the smirkers. I'm sure my multi-tasking was not a part of any PeaceKeeper protocols.

Bren chuckled, shaking his head. "There truly is no need to worry about your safety, is there?"

I grinned up at him. "I may be just a 3rd, but I'm a wily one! We authors are creative folk," I retorted. Then I sobered. "Linda is pretty shaken up, Bren. She had no idea she was being handled."

"Neither did we," he replied. "This new revelation is troubling."

"But you did sense it," I pointed out. "You knew something was off, you just hadn't known what. I'm sure if Mac hadn't been pressuring you, you would have discovered what it was." I shook my head. "These people, whoever they are, are getting out of control. How's Mac, Bren?"

Bren sighed. "Hurt. He feels betrayed."

I nodded sympathetically. "That's one good thing about Linda being handled. It means she did not betray him."

Bren had taken Mac directly to the Resuscitation chambers on Sal 5. Doc had not been there, but the technicians went right to work, creating a new corpus for Mac's seed atoms.

"We shall soon be facing another issue, my love," Bren said. "Word will get back to the Division heads that Mac, who was on leave, has been injured."

I nodded and sighed as I leaned against him.

"I never expected Mac to drop his shield," Bren said mournfully as he stroked my back. "It was the last order I gave him."

I barked out a laugh. "This, coming from someone who had a doctor use the last of a 9th's DNA to create a Silistel Corpus for a dying 3rd!"

His glanced down at me, brow furrowed. "That was different. I gave an order. Mac should have obeyed, but he did not. He dropped his shield."

I smiled and shook my head, "How is it different? Perhaps nobody told you not to create a Silistel corpus for me, but I'm willing to bet if they had known what you were planning to do, they would have." I nuzzled his neck. "It's called love, Bren." I said softly, "We all do crazy things for love. Doesn't matter if we're 3rds, 5ths, 7ths, or..." I shrugged, "...perhaps even 9ths. Who knows?"

Bren gathered me to him and I wrapped my arms more firmly around his waist, letting his warmth seep through me. He kissed the top of my head.

"I am so glad that love does make us do crazy things," I told him. "Because of you, we have us."

After a while I stirred. "What exactly happened back there, Bren? You froze."

He stiffened. "I did. I never have before. It was alarming." He withdrew from my embrace and began to pace the room, running fingers through his hair. "All I can say in my defense is the brutality of that attack shocked me into a profound stillness. I literally could not believe what I was witnessing." He shook his head as if clearing the memory. "Perhaps it is no longer appropriate for me to be a Keeper."

I went to him, forcing him to stop his pacing so I could hug him. "Perhaps you're simply allowing yourself to evolve?" I suggested.

Chapter 32 - Regrouping

We left the Waldorf well before dawn.

Bren decided we should leave Earth entirely, and stay at his cabin on Montorea until we had a better sense of what was happening. I took Linda directly to the cabin. Bren collected Ian, Langsford and Frankie from Kona so he could brief them. I'm sure they were worried, having been unable to connect with us for nearly twenty-four hours.

I'm glad I had a few moments with Linda before the others arrived so I could visit with her. She seemed tired and dazed. "You're holding up a heck of a lot better than I was when I learned about all this," I told her.

She rubbed her temples, "I can't quite believe I'm not on Earth," she said. She looked about her. "It doesn't look that much different."

"That's why I like it here—this cabin—it feels like home." I replied. "I haven't seen much else, other than a space station that looks like a set from *Star Wars* and a family's modern home that looked like it was plucked from Middle America." I sat down across from her and smiled. "Bren—

Captain Faulkner—has been allowing me to adjust slowly so I don't overload. It was all a tad overwhelming," I said wryly. "But I'm feeling pretty good now."

Linda nodded, "I'm lucky I have you to help me with this. It's a good thing I know these people as well though my psychic connection to Mac." Her face clouded over, lips trembling.

I touched her hand. "Mac will be fine."

She shook her head, "You don't understand. It took him a long time for him to trust me after he discovered he was being handled. We established a working relationship readily enough, but that was only because Mac trusted Captain Faulkner." Tears glistened in her eyes when she glanced at me. "Underneath his rough exterior, he is a very gentle soul. A beautiful soul." She blinked rapidly. "Although I do not remember what I did to him, he does. I'm afraid he will reject me," she whispered.

"Maybe at first, I'm not going to lie," I told her, "But I promise you I will talk sense into him."

Linda looked doubtful.

"I will make sure he hears me." I told her touching her arm, "You can count on me." I smiled, "I'm a sucker for a happy ending."

She would have said more, but it was at that moment Bren and the rest of the crew arrived.

It took longer than a mere touch for Bren and me to report our adventures to the others.

I felt badly when they made us aware of their anxious waiting. "I should have called," I said in apology.

"And we probably would not have known how to answer the telephone," Ian replied, making everyone laugh.

I knew they knew how to answer a simple phone call, and was grateful for his ability to lighten the mood.

"Now what?" asked Frankie, with a half-sigh, half-yawn. She looked pale and had dark rings under her eyes.

I glanced at the others who pretty much looked the same and was stung by guilt. Their sleepless night was mostly my fault. I could have brought Linda to Hawaii.

"Since you all look fairly motley," Bren said, "I suggest we take a short leave to rest up. Would three days appeal to everybody?"

They jumped on it.

"I'll take you all to Ian's, then. But before you go," Bren said, "I would like you to use my mem-unit to report your experiences on Earth."

He glanced at Ian.

"Regarding our freedoms, what is the climate, Brother?" he asked. "Should we proceed with caution? Are we still being watched?"

"Give me two hours and I will have an answer," he replied.

Bren nodded. "Time enough for you all to file reports," he said, handing his mem-unit to Frankie, "I've set it to record, just pass it around when you're done," he told her.

She nodded and went to the kitchen, the others trailing behind her.

I turned to Linda, "Do you know what a mem-unit is?"

I asked.

She shook her head and I went to the bedroom I shared with Bren and collected mine to explain what it did and how it worked. "This little guy," I said holding it up to her, "saved me from going stark raving mad."

Linda smiled and looked at it curiously.

"Would you mind if I recorded your memories?" I asked her. "Something may show up to help us learn how you became handled without your knowledge," I explained. Then I thought of an important question. "Did you have any headaches you recall?"

She shrugged, looking warily at my mem-unit, "I have headaches quite frequently. I refer to them as 'third eye aches,' because I get them from over-using my clairvoyance." She frowned at the unit. "Does it hurt?"

"Not at all," I said. "There is this pulling sensation that feels strange, but it doesn't hurt. I have my own because it's a great way to keep a journal. It records not only what you remember, but what your subconscious remembers as well. When I replay it, I'm amazed at how much I missed that my subconscious picks up. It's fascinating."

"It sounds fascinating," she replied unconvincingly as she cautiously reached for it. "If it will help you, I will do it."

I thanked her, and fitted the headset to her, making the necessary adjustments. "Now remember, there will be an odd pulling sensation, but it doesn't last long." I showed her how to stop and start the unit and then sat back to watch. "You're running the show," I told her. "You can always turn it off, but it will turn itself off on its own when you're done."

She paled slightly but smiled at me before she closed

her eyes. I watched as her fingers connected with the on button. I smiled when her body gave a little jump. I had done the same thing.

It only took about fifteen minutes, and she opened her eyes as soon as the unit turned itself off.

"How do you feel?" I asked her,

She brightened. "Much better," she replied with a smile. "Kind of like when I step out of the confessional." She looked at me. "I gave you everything, from the time of my recruitment until now."

"Wow, thank you," I said. "I've got a feeling this will be of considerable help."

I went to put the mem-unit back on my dresser, but then changed my mind, thinking Ian might have better luck deciphering the info.

When I returned to the living room, I found Linda gazing out the window.

"Would you like to go for a walk by the lake?" I asked her.

She turned, "I would love that," she said. "Being by water calms me."

"Out you go, then," I told her. "Just don't wander too far. Don't want you to get lost."

She smiled and nodded.

I watched her walk away, tall and willowy, thinking how self-contained she was. Then I went to find Ian.

He smiled when I approached.

"How's it going?" I asked him.

"The usual," he replied. "I've input my algorithms and am just waiting for the data. Another hour or so." He looked at me. "You?"

"I have some information for you in my mem-unit. Linda downloaded all her experiences, from the time she was hired through this morning. I think it could tell something, don't you?"

Just by looking at the gleam in Ian's eye, I had my answer. "Mind if I make a copy of it?" he asked.

I held up my unit. "I thought you'd never ask," I replied with a smile, handing it over to him after I had punched in my privacy code.

I watched him hook the device to another unit to transfer the data. He looked up. "When this is all over, I would like for you and Bren to stay with us for a long visit," he said. "Domena and I are so happy you are in Bren's life. Anyone who has brought the kind peace and happiness to my brother as you have will always be welcome." He paused. "And even if you and my brother were not together, Domena would welcome your company any time."

It was so heartfelt my throat closed and I could only nod and squeeze his shoulder in thanks.

Two and a half hours later, Ian gave us a thumbs-up to take our three-day leaves. As far as he could tell, it was business as usual with the Corps. The only information he found mentioning us were several encrypted messages between the Division heads. When he deciphered the codes, the information was very telling, and I knew Bren and I were going to have some interesting conversations in the very near future.

But first on my list was making things right between Linda and Mac.

Like I'd told Linda, I'm a sucker for a good old *happily ever after* ending.

Chapter 33 - Relationships are a Bitch

Bren had been gone the whole afternoon. Having dropped off the rest of the Five, he had lingered with Ian and enjoyed the visit with his family. The boys were settled and happy. Domena enjoyed her teaching, but he told me she had new worry lines etched about her eyes and mouth, which made me sad.

"It is not good for Ian to be away on a mission," Bren told me. "If we return to the Earth base, he will not be joining us." I nodded in agreement. "Domena asked about you," Bren continued with a smile. "She is anxious to visit with her new sister again."

I smiled back. "I've never had a sister," I told him. "How nice to be thought of as one."

In the kitchen, I heard Linda humming softly as she prepared our dinner.

When she had returned from her walk along the lake, she was much calmer, and she insisted she fix us a meal, telling me cooking helped her cope with her issues. From the smells beginning to filter into the living room, it promised to be a good meal.

"Think Mac is ready?" I asked Bren, nodding my head toward the kitchen.

Bren shook his head. "He will never be ready," he answered. "He is unhappy and closed. I haven't even told him she's with us. I believe it would only give him more time to build his wall."

I nodded, "What's your plan?"

Bren smiled, "We bring him here and mediate their first meeting."

I grimaced. "Oh, now, *this* should be fun."

Bren grinned. "I'll go get him after dinner, then?"

I took a big whiff of the lovely cooking smells. "Definitely after dinner," I said as my stomach rumbled.

* * *

"By the bloody winged balls of Mercury, I will not see her!" Came the shout from the other room. "*Ever!*"

Linda froze, her arms elbow-deep in soapsuds. We were in the kitchen, cleaning up after having enjoyed a lovely meal of roasted something. I didn't know the name of the little pig-like animal residing on this planet. But it sure was tasty, and Linda had cooked it perfectly.

"I think we should get in there," I told her, drying off the final plate. "That roasting pan needs to soak, anyway," I told her, handing her my dishtowel for her hands.

Saying nothing, she slowly rinsed and wiped her hands, her eyes getting wider as the shouting in the next room escalated.

"I don't care what the reason, the woman murdered me!"

Bren said something in a soothing murmur I didn't quite catch.

"Not if she were the last female sentient in the galaxy, Bren!" Mac shouted, "Holy winged bitches of Schraff, Bren! One last time, I. WILL. NOT. Oh!"

Mac stopped in mid-shout and stared murderously at Linda when we entered the room. He paled and pointed a finger at us, "Do not come a step closer!"

"And you!" he pointed a finger at me. "I thought we were friends!" Mac let his hand fall fisted at his side, panting his rage.

"I am your friend, Mac," I answered quietly as I sent tendrils of love and warmth to him.

He jerked and took a step back, waiving his hands in front of him, "And none of that energy stuff!" he growled. "I've been manipulated enough."

I stopped immediately. "I'm sorry, Mac, I only wanted to help you feel better."

"How can I feel better with *that* in the room?" He replied, glaring at Linda.

Linda gasped out a sob and hurried back into the kitchen.

I could hear her weeping.

"Mac," Bren said, looking at me, "she is an innocent," he said patiently.

This is what I've been dealing with for the past 30 minutes, I didn't even give him the option of coming down here. Just grabbed him.

He's got a pretty good mad going.

"She's no innocent, Bren," he spat back. "She murdered me."

"Mac," Bren repeated. "She is an innocent and we are PeaceKeepers."

I think it was Linda's sobbing in the background rather than Bren that restored Mac's reason.

"Mac," Bren persisted, "as I've said before, Linda was being handled. That makes her an innocent."

He looked at him blankly.

I sent thought to Bren. *Maybe something is getting through to him.*

It has taken long enough. I've never seen him act this way before.

Love does crazy things.

Bren hid his smile well.

"Handled?" Mac asked.

"She was being handled, Mac, and I made sure that handler would never invade another's mind again." I told him fiercely. "He was the one who killed you."

Mac blinked and his knees began to buckle. Bren caught his friend, guiding him to a chair and crouched beside him.

Mac wiped his face with his hand and looked up at Bren. "Handled? Linda?"

Bren nodded.

"Why didn't you tell me this sooner?"

Bren snorted. "I did, you stubborn fool, you just weren't ready to hear me."

We waited quietly while Mac processed the information, the only sounds being Linda's muffled sobs from the next room.

"And you took care of my murderer?"

"Oh yeah," and I told Mac all about my multi-tasking.

He nodded, "Just deserts. I thank you, angel."

After a few moments, Mac looked at Bren, his expression haggard. "I should have known, Bren. She'd begun to act differently, but I loved her too much to see it, I did." He sighed, "I've broken all kinds of protocols, Bren."

Bren clapped his hand on his friend's shoulder. "And I have not?" he said, nodding his head at me.

Mac smiled at me. "Hello, Angel." he said.

"Hello, Mac," I replied.

Mac gazed at the kitchen doorway. "I'd better go to her," he said.

"It would be the kind thing to do," I agreed.

He looked at Bren. "It's her, isn't it? Linda? No handler?"

Bren smiled. "No handler, Mac. Your angel made sure of that."

Mac clapped his hands on his knees and rose from the chair, "I best take care of her, then," he said as he headed towards Linda's sobs.

"We'll be right here if you need us," said Bren, rising with him.

Mac shot him a glance, "Oh, I think I have this one under control," he said.

Bren put an arm around my shoulder as we listened. Linda's sobs quieted for a moment and then resumed, but the energy had shifted from sorrow to joy.

I glanced at him and he smiled. "Shall we go to Hawaii?" he asked.

I nodded. "We probably should clean up the place and then check out."

"Perhaps," he said. "In three days' time."

He took my hand; we exited Montorea and entered Earth.

Immediately, I felt the difference.

I was home again.

"Now what?" I asked glancing up at him from under my lashes while playing with his shirt buttons.

Chapter 34 - Encrypted Messages

The place Bren and I had chosen as the safe house in Hawaii opened up to a deck. From the deck was a path to the beach. I found myself walking down the path, swim mask and flippers in hand. Bren had teleported back to Montorea to talk with Ian and to check on how Mac was doing. Since we still had two more days before the League of Five-plus-extras reconvened, I was determined to relax and enjoy myself.

Gotta say, Mac and Linda's reunion and my subsequent night with Bren had gotten me off to a good start.

I had finally done it. I had finally surrendered to Bren's gentle urging and opened completely to him, despite my fear. Only to find I had nothing to fear. Isn't that always how it is?

His mind did not come pouring into mine as I'd assumed. I did not merge with him, nor did I lose myself and disappear. No, my thoughts and feelings braided with his. Who we were remained a constant. It was amazing. There were no boundaries to our feelings, only acceptance and love. So much love. Oh, my God. There is no way I could possibly explain it to anybody. I'm not even sure a mem-unit could be up for the task. It would probably spontaneously combust.

I grinned, not caring I was glowing at the memory. Not caring about much about anything. I was filled with a fearless joy, rejoicing in all life. And full-blown-in-love-ness with Captain Brennar Faulkner, the sweetest and hottest man in the whole universe.

I left my towel and cover-up on a lava outcropping and continued my trek to the beach. The waves buffeted me as I sat on the ledge, fitting my flippers to my feet and adjusting my facemask. Putting the snorkel into my mouth, I slipped into the ocean, letting the surge take me a little distance from shore. I came up for air and then dove deeper, reveling in the sight of the bright schools of fish darting about as if of one mind. Looking below me, I saw a green turtle at a cleaning station, its mossy shell covered with little fish eating the turtle's shell clean. I turned my back on the shore and lay spread-eagled and facedown, breathing through my snorkel tube. In front of me was the deep turquoise of the ocean spreading out from light to dark as far as I could see. The ombre blue went on and on, splintered in places by the yellow sunbeams. Water gurgled in my ears and the rhythm of my breath balanced itself with the deep in and out pulls of the surge. I was warm. I was relaxed.

I surrendered.

Suddenly, I was a part of it all, and this time, because of the night before, I was fearless. My body seemed to have disappeared as I braided myself with everything: the turtle, the fish, the lava rocks, the ocean itself. I expanded farther and included my towel and cover-up, the beach house, the asphalt, the other beach houses....I kept expanding and expanding...never forgetting who I was, but including everything, literally everything. I expanded into cities and mountains, fire hydrants and the prayer flags of a Tibetan temple. I expanded into trees and the street lamp at my old apartment. In every direction, I reached out. To the moon. To the sun. The stars.

And then Bren was there. Bren and I were all things and we were each other. I looked at myself from his eyes and he looked at me from my own.

And then, I was lying, spread-eagled and face down in the deep blue, listening to the rhythmic cycle of my breath through the snorkel tube as it aligned itself to the ocean surge.

And I was no longer alone. I would never be alone again.

I would never be afraid again.

I righted myself, raised my swim mask so I could see Bren more clearly, and spat out my snorkel tube.

"Wow," I said.

He smiled his dimpled smile.

* * *

I rinsed off the salt and wrapped my body in a robe and my hair in a towel. Bren was sitting on the deck eating a bowl of cereal. There was a bowl waiting for me, filled with granola and fresh fruit: mangos, bananas and kiwi. I frowned at the kiwi, and then tucked into my breakfast.

"I brought the decoded messages between Major General Carringdon and Lt. General LeFlow," he said. "Perhaps we should look at them."

I chewed and swallowed. "After we eat?" I asked, savoring the flavors.

He took another bite and nodded at me, his eyes

crinkling at the corners. *You realize,* he thought, *if we communicate thusly, we can continue to eat.*

True, but then, I'd be distracted from my food, this view and you.

I felt his laughter.

We crunched our granola together in silence, enjoying the perfumed scent of the heavy, damp air. I knew something in those transmissions was bothering him, but I put it aside and relaxed, enjoying myself.

When done, we rose in unison and went inside. I rinsed our bowls and left them in the kitchen sink. In the bedroom, I put on a bathing suit top and the bright green board shorts Frankie had bought me, throwing on an oversized T-shirt with the emblem of the Emissaries of Evolution a fan had sent me. I towel-dried my hair, grabbed a hairbrush and went back to the dining table where Bren had laid out the messages between Carringdon and LeFlow. I sat beside him and began to work at the rat's nests in my hair as I scanned the table.

"Paper," I said. "How quaint!" I put my brush down and picked up a sheet.

Bren shrugged and picked up the brush, "Ian's technology at his home did not blend with Earth's," he said as he began to tackle my tangles.

"Mmmm," I replied, already focusing on the correspondence, I shot Bren a glance. "Have you read any of this?" I asked reaching for another page.

He nodded. "All of it."

I gestured at the pages in my hand. "They think I'm dangerous, Bren!"

He nodded quietly, "They know nothing of you, Rose."

I picked up a third page, my eyes widening. "They no longer trust you as well!" I said, reading, "*The quantum entanglement between the 3rd who hosted Captain Faulkner's seed atoms and Captain Faulkner leads me to believe they should both be considered rogue anomalies.*" I huffed. "Rogue anomalies! What the heck does that mean?"

"It means they have no idea what the limits of our capabilities are and are being cautious," Bren answered, setting the brush down and running his finger through my curls.

I closed my eyes, sharing my pleasure through our connection.

He kissed my neck. *If you keep doing that, my Rose, we will never leave this place.*

"I could think of worse things to happen," I purred. "Besides, you started it by brushing my hair."

Bren stopped, wrapping his arms about my waist instead, his chin on my head.

With a sigh, I picked up the last page and continued reading, my thoughts refocusing.

"Ohmigod!" I looked up at him, "Langsford's spying for them? They're behaving just like the people they're trying to contain here on Earth." I put the papers back on the table and Bren loosened his arms so I was able to turn and look at him. "What a mess."

Bren nodded, "The whole system appears skewed."

"It appears wacko. Too bad we can't send every last one of them through rehab!"

"A shame, Rose," he said drolly.

I shook my head, "How different this is compared to what we experienced this morning." I said, "Too bad we can't share that with them," I mused. I felt myself glowing. "It was different from last night, but similar, huh?"

Even Bren started glowing at last night's memory before he refocused on topic.

"This morning, we united with…" his voice trailed off and he sent me images and feelings instead of trying to describe what had happened to us, what we had shared with ourselves and whatever we had chosen to share.

I shook my head woefully. "I don't think they would unite with us like that. I think your Division heads are too afraid."

"But Lt. General LeFlow is a 7th!" he answered, shaking his head, baffled.

I shrugged. "Doesn't seem to matter. She's not thinking on a very evolved level right now," I said, gesturing to the pages strewn on the table.

I sighed. "Maybe if we spoke to her. If she could relate to us not as Lieutenant. General LeFlow, but as a 7th, she would feel more at ease," I said musingly. "I mean, you and I…neither of us would ever deliberately hurt anyone."

Bren looked thoughtful. "I believe we should visit LeFlow as soon possible," he told me. "Perhaps we should give her a taste of what you discovered we could do this morning. The…" he reached for the words to describe the indescribable, smiled and looked at me helplessly.

"The Indescribable Happy?" I suggested.

He flashed his dimple. "That will do."

I grinned back. "Once she experiences it, she'll see. And I don't believe we should ask her, Bren. I think we should just go ahead and show her, just gather her up like we gathered everything up this morning."

Chapter 35 - We Are At War Here, People

It was late afternoon at the Guardian headquarters on Montorea. Bren and I thought that would be the best time to visit LeFlow, since most people would be on their way home.

We stood outside LeFlow's office door and I, for one, was glad the corridor was empty. I stood out, wearing my bright green board shorts, flip-flops, bathing suit top and tee. Not quite military dress code. Bren was wearing some off-duty coverall thingy and boots. It was a hideous mustard color, but it showed off his physique so well I allowed him to wear it anyway. I also allowed him to walk in front of me so I could enjoy the showing off of said physique.

We both gently extended our senses and knew LeFlow was behind the door, alone and very much aware we were there. She was also uncertain and a little afraid. I opened a little more fully and sent her a greeting, let her see my frame of mind, that I wasn't some maniacal Frankenstein monster.

With our senses extended, we felt when she had decided to let is in.

That was when we knocked.

The door swished open and she beckoned to us.

LeFlow was the first full-on 7th I had met face to face. I didn't consider the last time I'd seen her as actually meeting her. She seemed lighter somehow, still very solid, but lighter, so much more than her physical body.

Bren was like that at times, more and more so, come to think of it. I wondered what impression I gave.

She was tall, elongated, graceful, and elegant, with eyes a little too large for her face, very much like a human on Earth, but that sense of not-quite-being-solid would have been noticed. And the big Japanese anime eyes. They still creeped me out. I could see why 7ths were Watchers, rather than Keepers or Guardians.

Despite her initial misgivings, LeFlow was calm, happy to see Bren, and curious about me. While I had been sizing her up, she had been scanning me as well. But she gave nothing away.

She reached out and touched us both. "Come," she said, and we followed her to the little alcove with the view of her garden and water feature I remembered from the mem-unit.

LeFlow cleared her throat. "I have concerns," she said.

"We know," Bren replied. "That is why we're here."

I let Bren lead us into the Indescribable Happy this time. It was like watching an artist weave completely different textures together from a small individual point—himself—expanding and gathering more and more. All these different things were combined and pulled along the wake of the force he had created.

First there was Bren, and then he gathered me with

---

him. Then LeFlow, followed by the sound of her waterfall, and then outward to the mechanisms of the shuttle system that took the small crafts back and forth to Sal 5, adding two guards talking about the women they had bedded, and then a chef on Montorea planning his next day's menu, to a pet dog-like creature, to the cabin Bren owned, bringing along Mac and Linda as they were making love, flowers and birds, the very core essence of Montorea, then outwards, to the stars and other planets, and the deep silence of space, itself. On and on, animate and inanimate, Bren gathered, braided and unified and distilled along the path he had created to the Indescribable.

It was so different from what I had woven. I realized there were infinite ways to create this journey. We expanded and unified until all that existed was that one, united, Indescribable.

Slowly and gently, Bren disengaged from us, allowing each, both animate and inanimate, those things of creation he had chosen to combine into the Journey he had carried us through, until we were each once more individuated and separated from each other, yet never separate.

LeFlow opened her eyes and gazed at each of us in wonder.

"Welcome to our world," I told her.

She smiled, the Indescribable Happy reflected in her eyes, her marvelously creepy eyes.

* * *

It takes a few moments to recover from an experience like that. Bren and I silently communed as LeFlow regrouped.

Do you realize how different each journey will be? I asked

389

him.

Infinite.

Forever.

And we will only get better at it, Bren.

Yes, we will, Rose.

Wow.

Indeed.

"What a remarkable experience," LeFlow said quietly.

Bren smiled, "And now you know we are not beings you need fear."

She nodded, eyes shining.

I shot a glance at Bren and then looked at LeFlow. "May we speak of Earth?" I asked her. "We have been staying there."

She nodded, "I have learned of this."

"Major General Langsford, yes, we know," Bren replied.

"Ahhh," she said, not totally surprised. "We would have been forced to stop you if you had interfered further."

I smiled at her sadly. "I sincerely doubt could have been able to stop us. I think you know that."

She sighed, studying me. "You are very young, are you not, little one? In the proper hands, persuasion and reason are a very powerful weapons."

"I'll keep that in mind," I replied frostily, shifting in my chair.

"Perhaps," she said, "if you understood why we feel

Earth is our responsibility."

I was about to reply I knew all of that and it didn't make any difference to me, but Bren touched my hand.

We should listen to what she has to say.

I sighed and nodded at him as I settled back in my chair and waited.

LeFlow glanced at Bren, sending him a brief smile. "I will assume you know of our past relationship with Earth," she said to me.

"That renegade PeaceKeepers took over the planet, messed with the DNA and ruled over the people as gods? Yes, I do know," I answered.

"And of course you know the PeaceKeeper Corps is currently struggling to recover from being attacked from within by these same Misaligned Ones?"

"I thought you *had* recovered," I said.

She nodded. "To the degree we have blocked their way into our midst, yes. However, given the recent attack upon Sergeant MacDougall, they clearly are not quelled. They will attempt another means. We cannot allow this," she said quietly.

I shook my head, confused. "What do you mean?"

"The PeaceKeeper Corps—indeed, our whole civilization—is extremely vulnerable simply because we have evolved beyond the frequencies of a 3rd. Since we are beyond their frequencies, we must rely on our technologies to translate the intentions of the 3rds. Since we are controlling the algorithms used to interpret the minds of a 3rd, there is always a percentage of error. It cannot be helped, but it can be contained.

"Our experience with the Misaligned Ones and Earth," she continued, "is a perfect example of our blind spot. The whole episode was misunderstood, and in 2000 years, that misunderstanding—the belief we had contained them—has led us to where we are at this very moment."

She paused, "And it is with regret we cannot allow this to progress further."

At her tone, all my senses shot to attention. "What do you mean by that?" I asked, narrowing my eyes.

Not waiting for her answer I looked at Bren. His face was grim.

"What does she mean by that?" I asked him as he reached for my hand.

LeFlow took a breath. "We are doing what we should have done in the beginning," she said sadly. "Rather than supporting their Awakening, an ARK has been launched and will contain the damage. Those sentients who have already been Awakened will be removed from the planet."

I tore my hand from Bren's grasp and rose from my chair, barely able to breathe. "What. Do. You. Mean?" I asked again.

LeFlow ignored me. Speaking to Bren, she continued. "We can solve this issue very quickly. It will not be taking 50 years to travel to Earth. There is a jump gate not far from Montorea we had closed off after we collected those Misaligned Ones for rehabilitation. The slipstream is extremely fast. The ARK will reach Earth in a matter of days."

"Bren," I said, still standing with clenched fists, "What is this….this…creature telling us?"

Bren sighed and reached for my hand, sending soothing energy to me. "I believe she is saying they plan to destroy Earth. That the ARK is already underway."

I felt the blood draining from my face and forced myself to sit down and breath.

"No! Bren!" I looked at him wildly, into his calm gaze.

He smiled at me, "And of course we will not allow that," he said soothingly. "They will simply contact the ARK and have it return."

"It's too late," said LeFlow. "The ARK has already gone through the gate and is in InnerSpace."

I began to expand with rage. LeFlow's eyes widened in fear. Perhaps, being a 7th, she did not recognize the emotion, but it was fear. And I stoked her fear, breathing into it as if it were an ember.

LeFlow paled. "Make her stop," she gasped at Bren.

"I will not," he answered. "You have called this to you. We have created her. We have all created her."

"Help me!" LeFlow pleaded to him. "My mind! It burns!"

Rose?

The Department heads, Bren, tell her to gather them. I need to leave before I do something I'll regret. I flashed him an image of the cabin. *I'm getting help.*

He understood.

I left.

Chapter 36 - Help

It was quiet, out in the middle of the lake. I stopped paddling and just allowed the boat Bren had made to drift at will. I sat back off the seat and looked up at the sky, feeling the warmth of an alien sun on my face as an alien breeze tousled my curls, bringing with it exotic scents I couldn't name.

It was all restful, peaceful and beautiful.

But it wasn't home.

It wasn't Earth.

I thought about what Bren had noted on his mem-unit about Planet-Striders and Sky-Riders. He was right. Earth will always be my home. I couldn't bear to think of my civilization—my home—being destroyed on account of a group of misaligned alien *dipshits* who thought they had the answer to raising consciousness.

"Bastards! Fucking bastards!" I hissed through clenched teeth.

I would not let that happen.

No, I absolutely would not.

Remembering my purpose, I took a deep breath, counted to ten, and then let it out slowly, closing my eyes. With great difficulty, I drew peace from my surroundings and meditated to the sound of the water softly slapping on the side of the little boat. When my mind had quieted enough, I let myself expand and I reached out an invitation to the 9th who had shared its DNA, bracing myself for the electrical impact I had remembered from Bren's experience.

But it didn't happen that way.

As Bren had described, I'd felt it coming long before it arrived. I opened my eyes to watch as it materialized across from me, bright and shining. When it was fully formed, it reached out soft and gentle tendrils that flowed through me. I was overcome with such a sense of profound joy, I just wanted to sink into it, never to return.

"Greetings, Little Sister," it said to me.

I gasped, focusing my eyes so I could see beyond the brightness to the being, itself. "I didn't know you could speak," I said in astonishment. "This wasn't how Bren experienced it."

The 9th shimmered with laughter. "You are Little Sister, not Little Brother. Is it so unusual? Do you greet all you know in the same manner?"

The joy bubbled through me, and I laughed as I answered, "No, I guess I don't."

"We are all the same, yet we are all different, do you agree?"

I nodded.

"*This one* is joyful to be called by you, yet *this one* is also curious why Little Sister has called."

"I want to know what I am and how I can help my Earth," I answered, again struggling to maintain my frequency levels so I could remain at a par with the 9th. "I thought perhaps you could help me with that."

"You are Little Sister, a part of the Divine Design." It paused, responding to my befuddlement. "*This one* sees you are not understanding that All is a part of the Divine Design."

"No, I don't understand. I don't understand at all. My body wasn't supposed to be like this. It wasn't planned. Bren had my seed atoms transferred into this body because I was dying and he wanted me to be safe. And," I added, "because he did not want to be the only one, and because he loves me."

"This happening does not mean you are not part of the Divine Design," the 9th replied. "There are infinite melodies the All applies to the One Creation. You and Little Brother have already experienced some of this when you blend with otherness. Little Sister, know each unique melody is played when the time IS for it to play. Soon it will be your time; yours and Little Brother's, together. When *this one* last visited with Little Brother, it was unclear how the song was to be sung. But *this one* stepped back far enough to see the way of this melody. It is very beautiful. Little Sister and Little Brother are very beautiful."

"But how can I be? I'm just a 3rd."

"*This one* does not understand what Little Sister is asking."

I paused, carefully selecting my words, I continued. "I am told I am an Awakening 3rd. The level of frequency I am

Awakening into is that of a 5th. The level of frequency a 5th will awaken into will be a 7th. A 7th will awaken into a 9th. When you compare my level of frequency to that of a 5th or the higher ones, I am lacking the knowledge and awareness they possess. I am Awakening, and they are already Awake."

The 9th's laughter shimmered through me.

"Little Sister lacks no knowledge." It explained, shimmering with laughter again. "Little Sister simply must reach out and ask. Nothing is inaccessible to Little Sister. Nothing is inaccessible to any of the very many expressions of the All.

"But I thought it was all levels of frequencies," I said. "The differences between us…3rds, 9ths, 5ths, 7ths. I thought we had to reach certain levels of awareness before we could understand more. I thought we had to be Awakened."

"Habits of thought," replied the 9th. "How can there be differences when all comes from All? All is always awake."

I twisted one of my curls. "So…" I said slowly, willing myself to understand, "…the 5ths and the 7ths have it wrong? There are no differences between what I am and what a 7th is or, you, or even an Unawakened One?"

"Habits of thought," the 9th answered. "Infinite ways of looking at the All. Infinite ways of expressing the All. Infinite ways of breathing *with* the All. "

"Breathing with the All," I repeated

"Sharing the same breath," the 9th told me, "But knowing who breathed the First Breath. Always remember who breaths the First Breath. That knowing is sometimes forgotten."

"And habits of thought keep this breathing from

happening?

"Impossible to keep the breathing from happening. Habits of thought are the resultant structures of breathing one way. Habits of thought were never created to be permanent things—can never become permanent things. They must shift and change to the motion of the breath. You and Little Brother are new breaths, bringing new ways of shifting and restructuring the current habits of thought, new breaths breathing with still newer breaths." The 9th paused. "Can you breathe with the All?" It asked.

The words seemed to be layered with so many meanings my mind could not wrap itself around them all. Perhaps, given time, but not right in that moment. I just felt there was more to those simple words than I was able to fathom.

Frustrating.

"I will do my best," I answered the 9th, "To breath with the All."

"And it will be a beautiful breath, a beautiful melody," it told me. "Shall we Blend?"

And with that, I became absorbed into a union with— for lack of a better word—my Parent. It was an experience I had only felt within the Indescribable Happy, but much more intense. My body orgasmed, so complete was the joy and the ecstasy. I was so startled I almost withdrew.

"Habits of thought," kept repeating as my mind mingled with the 9th.

"Habits of thought," I agreed, and laughed.

* * *

"The 9ths call it Blending," I told Bren, bursting into the cabin. "The Indescribable Happy, they call Blending."

He reached for me and I began to transfer all I had experienced.

"We can do this, Bren!" I exclaimed, renewed and filled with certainty. *"We can stop them."*

"Then let us begin. I'm sure they've gathered by now."

Chapter 37 - Earth's Ambassador

"I apologize if our methods are distressing you," Carringdon stated calmly. "Nevertheless, the ARK has been dispatched and will reach your Earth as scheduled."

"And it can easily be un-dispatched," I said, slowly rising to my feet, my indignation flowing out into the room. "Otherwise, Bren and I will teleport to that ARK and make them stop."

"But it is in InnerSpace." The Major General replied with finality. "You are too late."

"I beg to differ, Blue Lady," I replied. "Don't you know by now Bren and I can do anything? That we are unstoppable?"

I saw Carringdon's eyes flicker with uncertainty. She looked at Bren, "Captain Faulkner, this is your creation. Please contain her."

Bren leaned back in his chair and crossed his arms. "I think not," he told her, as he reached for my hand, our fingers naturally interlacing.

"Wh—!!" she exclaimed. I felt the heat of her anger raging towards me, unaware of what she—a 5th—was feeling.

The 9th had opened my eyes. Their belief in these frequency evolutions was all just habits of thought. There was no Awakening process. There was no progression from one frequency level to another that took millions of years. There were no misconceptions or misalignments between those frequency levels. Everything was available to all creation at any time.

Just habits of thought keeping things as they were.

Habits could be broken.

LeFlow gently laid a hand on Carringdon's arm. "Perhaps we should listen to her." She smiled at me tremulously, respectful of my power.

"Thank you," I told her, displaying the dignity I felt an Ambassador of Earth should display. Because, despite the fact I was still wearing my board shorts, swimsuit top and tee, that is how I thought of myself. I took a deep breath.

"Let me tell you a story from my perspective," I began.

"You have just discovered your protocols are not going to work on Earth," I told them. "You have reasoned since the PeaceKeeper Corps is comprised entirely of 5ths and 7ths, you see everything from that point of view." I smiled. "I don't expect you to fully understand what I am about to say. After all, I am a mere 3rd."

I held up my hand to stop Carringdon from speaking. "You have decided," I continued, raising my voice a bit, "that no matter how deep your cover will be, no matter how many thousands of years you have studied us, you can never EVER pretend to be us. It's impossible!"

I paused, letting that sink in. "Therefore, you have determined the Earth must be destroyed. Why? Because your enemy knows you and you do not know your enemy. This is not about PeaceKeepers coming in and midwifing Awakening 3rds. This is about PeaceKeepers coming to a planet where you are known, expected and unwanted because those Misaligned Ones are still there.

"These renegade PeaceKeepers who began all this…they were part of you. They do not want to have the sentients Awaken, even if the rest of the planet does. They know who you are, they know how you operate, and they've had a couple of thousand years to prepare for your coming. Oh, and you will be arriving on their home turf. Therefore, you have determined you must destroy the Misaligned Ones once and for all before you are destroyed." I paused, looking at the blue lady. "How am I doing? Is that about right?"

"Yes, you have summarized the events correctly," she replied.

I laughed. "Gee, that sounds just like the paranoid reasoning of a 3rd."

I gathered them all up within my mind, so quickly they could not react beyond a jolt of fear I thought fitting for what I was about to do.

"I am the Ambassador of Earth and now I am going to show you Earth," I told them. "I am going to show you so-called…" I spat the word, "*PeaceKeepers* just exactly what you have done to us with your 2000 years of interference."

And I did.

I showed it all to them. I united us, bound us all together and took them on a journey, not to the Indescribable

Happy—no, not that....but something else indescribable—its absence.

We went into the minds of the fearful and the hateful, the condemned waiting on death row, greedy pimps beating their whores and getting them addicted to crack, the addicts and the homeless, those who had given up with living, those who planned murder, those in the midst of battle lust, those who were raping children and then killing them, those who were impregnating terrified young girls, filling their bodies with babies and diseases.

I felt the horrified reactions of those I held in my mind, their struggles to be released from my grip, but I only tightened it and forced them to see more and more. Over and over I savaged them with images and sensations—cries in the night, pleas of the condemned, hopelessness, anger, death. I showed them the mind games that had been installed in the leaders, the myths and lies—complements of the so-called PeaceKeepers—that had taken hold of and shaped the leaders of the secret societies, poisoning all those that were touched, filling them with paranoia and plotting.

And at last, sensing the surrender and deep despair of those PeaceKeepers I had bound to me, I took pity. I showed the shining ones who, out of these horrors, turned their backs on the offal, who had overcome their fear and fought back against their oppressors with peace—the Ghandis, the Martin Luther Kings, the John Lennons. Those who somehow knew there *was* a better way to be and kept searching for it, searching until they, or their children, or others in their sphere of influence, found that other way of being. I showed them how the shift was happening, on its own and despite the efforts of the others, the misaligned and tainted ones who had been nurtured on lies.

And from here, I made a U-turn, sending us all into the natural progression of life within the forests, the sea, and into the welcoming joy of a pod of killer whales, who evolved, untouched and unshaped, into beings who were both wild animals joyfully hunting in packs, and beings steeped in ancient wisdoms. *Who Awakened these ones?* I whispered into their minds.

I took them higher and higher as we went deeper and deeper into union, into that Indescribable Place. And right before I released them so we could reemerge into our own selves, I showed them one last image: a young mother, sitting on a porch swing, rocking and singing softly to her nursing child as she watched the flicker of fireflies winking across her lawn.

"Call back the ARK," I said, looking around at their shocked and pale faces, drained by their emotions. "Bren and I will fix this."

"What will you do?" whispered Carringdon.

Chapter 38 - The New League of Five

"We will create peace," Bren answered gently, lovingly, as he rose to stand beside me.

He touched their minds, those minds I had so recently filled with images of horror and despair, erasing the pain and leaving only peace.

They gave a collective sigh.

"The ARK was instructed to contact us as soon as it comes out of InnerSpace and through the gate," a haggard Carringdon told me, her face a pale blue. "We will order them to return to Montorea."

I smiled and bowed. "Thank you," I said. I looked into each of their faces. "Thank you all. I do not apologize for my behavior. However, I promise I will not take you there again."

I glanced at Bren and he nodded. "We're going now," I said. "But before we do, I wanted to pass something on a wise 9th recently told me."

I paused. "It said we should never forget who it was that breathed the First Breath."

***

Mac and Linda were already at the cabin when we arrived. Bren contacted the rest of the League of Five, telling them to find their own means of travel. We both just wanted to be together quietly. As we waited outside for them to arrive, we wandered down to the dock and sat, leaning against one another for support. I slid my arm around his waist.

"Was I too harsh with them?" I asked.

"It was something they needed to know," he answered.

I nodded, satisfied, and we were silent.

"When do we get to go to Astragon 7?" I asked.

He grinned at me, a deep-dimple grin. "Soon," he said.

"I want to sit in that hidey-hole you discovered when you were young." I glanced down at myself. "I think I'm small enough."

"You are."

"I hope we dock at Gate 9."

"More than likely."

"By the sun-drenched balls of the stony Ferlew!" exclaimed Mac from behind. "It's good to see you all!"

"The rest of the League has arrived," Bren said dryly.

I snickered.

We went to greet them.

Mac, Linda, Frankie, Ian and Langsford stood in a row, waiting for us. I smiled. Mac was right. It was good to see them all, even our spy.

"Did you think Bren wouldn't find out?" I asked Langsford.

"I was a soldier following orders," he replied, a little reservedly.

"Don't worry, we're not planning on blowing your cover," I told him. "But you should," I said looking pointedly at Frankie.

Frankie glanced up at Langsford in confusion.

"Later," he told her, patting her hand and looking pointedly back at me.

Bren filled them in on everything that had happened from the time we read the deciphered correspondence between LeFlow and Carringdon to my little conversation with the Division heads.

They answered with varying degrees of silence.

"What now?" Linda asked timidly into the silence. "Will I be able to go home?"

Mac put an arm about her and held her close.

"As I told the heads," answered Bren, "Rose and I will make peace."

"And then what?" asked Ian, softly.

"And that's where you all come in," he replied. "I have an idea. Shall we go inside and sit around the table and science it through?"

When we were settled, Bren began.

"Suppose the seven of us were to go to Earth, in a ship, out in the open, and introduce ourselves."

"We'd be blown out of the sky," Langsford said. "I

don't see how that will create peace."

Bren chuckled and glanced at me. "Rose and I have another option," he told them. "First we will open their minds a bit."

"You'll Awaken them?" asked Frankie.

"No, not that," he said. "However, we will give them the desire to Awaken."

"How?" asked Mac.

"By showing them a taste of this," I answered happily, looking at Bren. "My turn?"

He nodded.

I took us on a short journey, gathering from their memories special places from the planets or space stations they called home. Collectively, we swirled and danced to the Indescribable Happy, and back again.

Regaining my physicality, I opened my eyes and looked at the others.

Ian shook his head, and wiped the tears of joy from his face. "That should do it," he said. "When can we go again?"

Mac laughed weakly.

Frankie gripped Langsford's hand with a knowing expression.

Bren smiled. "You just experienced what my Rose has named the Indescribable Happy."

They all looked at me and I sat, arms folded and just shrugged. "I'm the author, here," I told them smugly. "I get to do the naming."

I knew that name Indescribable Happy was simple and

trite. In fact, the more I used it and shared it with others, the more trite and unworthy it seemed as a way to describe such a beautiful and profound experience.

It gave me a giggle, though, to think of some of serious folks like Major General Carringdon, Leader of Division A explaining to Brigadier General Tomal, Leader of Division B, how Captain Faulkner had taken them to the Indescribable Happy. Maybe I should shorten it to the "Big Happy." That would be even funnier. I decided to run that by Bren when we had the time.

"We will make it quite a production, too," I said, looking at Linda. "Like something from Disneyland."

Feeling better, she laughed, "Please not the *It's A Small, Small World* ride."

I cocked my head at her. "Perhaps just use the music?"

She groaned.

"And after we introduce ourselves?" Langsford asked, steering us back to the subject.

"Rose called herself an Ambassador of Earth, and I thought perhaps we could be Ambassadors of…" He looked at me.

"The Ambassadors of the Interstellar Family," I said without hesitation.

"Perfect." Bren said.

"What would we do, Bren?" asked Ian

"We would use our collective skills to teach them a new way of being, "he said. "For example, you could teach them the new technologies the Watchers use. And Domena could bring members of the Artisan Guilds to spread new ways of creating."

"And Mac, Frankie and I could teach our PeaceKeeping methods," said Langsford, enthusiastically.

"Add some history of Earth in there," I said. "We all have a right to know that."

"What if they resist?" said Langsford.

"Then Rose and I will take them on another journey..."

"To the Big Happy," I said, testing out my new name. "Over and over, as needed." I decided to keep it Indescribable.

Mac leaned over to Linda. "If they're smart, they'll resist," he said in a stage whisper.

"What of the Resuscitation chambers?" asked Linda. "Would that be offered to our sick and dying?"

I remembered what the 9th had told me: All was available to All, but it wasn't my place to say that. This was Bren's creation. He was the one breathing the Breath.

"With compassion and patience, all things should be available," he answered. "Perhaps not at first. It would likely overwhelm them. But with time, all we know will be shared."

One of the many reasons I loved him, I thought.

"This will take some planning," said Ian.

"And help and cooperation from your Divisions," I said skeptically.

"I'll handle it," said Langsford.

And I heard the truth in his words.

Chapter 39 - The Peace Makers

Bren has this stance I call his Clint Eastwood look. He crosses his arms and stands with one hip cocked and his head a little to the side, with one eyebrow slightly lifted. And he waits, quietly staring at his target with those "I've got you in my sights" blue, blue eyes.

That's what he did now, with all the Division heads.

We were in a meeting, the early planning phases of Operation Earth Rescue (my label, of course), and they were squabbling like a bunch of kids. These people had been in their positions for so long apparently they had forgotten good leaders were also good followers.

But I shouldn't be too harsh with them. Bren and I were pushing their comfort zones and pushing pretty hard.

Earth was imploding, and something had to be done fast to stop them from self-destructing. From what the Watchers were reporting, it looked like all the information the fear-mongers had been feeding the people for centuries was turning against them. Those who were naturally Awakening were sensitive enough to be aware of where the ungrounded fears were coming from, and they were going for the jugular. Nobody likes to learn they had been lied to for centuries. It was getting messy and promising to get messier.

411

And for all their protocols, the PeaceKeepers had nothing to guide them through this particular planet's Awakening. Normally, they were there to midwife an Awakening world and guide those sentients into a more peaceful way of life. This time, the midwives had discovered the baby was breeched, and they, the PeaceKeeper midwives, needed to perform an emergency C-section or the Awakeners would all die. Earth's Awakening, which was already in progress, would have to be an aggressive one. And nobody relished the prospect of doing what Bren and I had proposed, especially the two of us.

What we were proposing was not guiding. What we were proposing was an intervention. But if we did not intervene, Earth would destroy itself. Those Awakening had no guidance. Those resisting the Awakening were fighting it with all their might. Personally, I'd prefer to be part of an intervention leading to recovery than be the one to send in an ARK to wipe them all out.

But first, it had been necessary for me to mend some fences with the Division heads

By way of an apology, I took them on an especially beautiful and soothing Indescribable Happy journey. After the nightmare ride I forced on them the first time, it was a miracle it took them only a few of moments to trust me enough to relax and enjoy the ride. I still did not regret my actions, but I had frightened them badly, so I didn't have to fake my gratitude for their renewed trust in me.

After a few moments of Bren's Eastwood, Major General Carrington stopped in mid-squabble, which caused the others to quiet down as well.

"Based on my brother's reports, I'd say we are wasting

time," Bren said quietly, "and will lose our opportunity to right a great wrong."

He paused to switch gears.

"Now, I would like the PeaceKeepers to prepare for the aftermath of Rose's and my intervention. I don't know how long it will take, but once Earth has achieved enough stability, and has adjusted to our presence, we need to be ready to bring them into the Collective as per our protocols."

"To clarify, Captain, do you mean we should use the same protocols used for any planet once the Awakening stage has been completed?" asked LeFlow.

Bren nodded. "Exactly. Once the fear has abated, then curiosity will prevail."

He glanced at Langsford. "I've asked Major General Langsford to coordinate the League of Five, the Keepers, and the Guardians. Captain Pritikin will assist him. "

Frankie opened her mouth to protest, but, being a good soldier, snapped it shut and shot Langsford a calculating look. She had been devastated when Langsford confessed he had been spying on us. He had tried to reassure her his feelings for her were the real deal, but she was holding off. Based on the look she gave Langsford, it appeared, although she was softening, she was still planning to make him grovel a bit.

I caught her eye and nodded my approval.

She smirked.

"My brother, Ian," Bren continued, "will fill the same position with the Watchers, and I would like you," he nodded to Pippa LeFlow, "Lieutenant General, to work with Domena Faulkner and her fellow Artisans. Their gifts, particularly those of the Harmonists, should provide immensely valuable support for Earth's transition. I would also like to get the other sentients on the planet involved."

"Oh, I would love to meet the other sentients," LeFlow exclaimed. "It has been such a long time since Watchers were able to work planetside during these early stages. Thank you, Captain Faulkner."

He nodded an acknowledgement. "Sergeant MacDougall and the Earth woman, Linda Carmichael, will be working closely with Rose and me. In addition, I would like Doctor Gauge to accompany us so he can help establish more advanced healing facilities," Bren said before turning his attention to the last two Division heads, Carrington and Tomal. "As for you two, Earth is not the only planet under PeaceKeeper care. I can think of none better to attend to the other missions," he said. "It has never been my intention to be anything other than a Captain in the PeaceKeeper Corps."

Tomal grunted. "So noted, Captain," he said, adding, "I am quite eager to observe how you resolve this particular crisis."

"Perhaps we can use your, uh, special skills for the other planets tainted by the Misaligned Ones from Earth," suggested Major General Carrington, although her suggestion had the flavor of a command.

Bren was noncommittal. "Perhaps," was all he said. Privately he directed a thought at me, *"Free will, Rose. It is easy to forget, when one is determined to help others Awaken, am I right?"*

"Very easy, my love," I answered in kind. *"So hard to allow others their choices."*

"Then we are in agreement we will only intervene this one

time."

"And only because this seems to be the only option."

As for the League of Five plus others, they all had plenty of challenges to address in addition to monitoring preparations and modifying protocols to fit this particular situation.

My personal concern was how to explain my re-emergence into life on Earth, with the added excitement of my storybook character, Joss Walker, living and breathing at my side. The minute the PeaceKeepers made themselves known with maximum exposure, it would be only a matter of time before I was identified.

"Perhaps we can use it to our advantage, instead," Ian mused when I voiced my concerns. "Let me run some algorithmic scenarios and get back to you."

Bren shot me a look of amusement. "He won't stop until he does make it work to our advantage," he chuckled.

As for the two of us, Bren and I had our own questions to answer. First and foremost was, just how much Indescribable Happy could a paranoid planet absorb before they became either terrified or addicted to the feeling? And whom should we target first?

My solution was to gather up all sentient beings that were already Awakened and escort them on a journey to the limits of their ability to integrate. After that, we could pair them up with as many Keepers and Artisans as possible for the rest of their integration process.

Bren, on the other hand, felt it was best to work with those in charge of the secret societies and hidden governments, the powers behind the thrones. But I thought that bunch should be thrust en masse into rehab chambers. It had worked so well with Linda Carmichael, why not them, I reasoned. Bren patiently explained it was against all PeaceKeeping protocols.

"But we are creating our own protocols anyway, Bren," I'd pointed out, and he really couldn't argue with me on that one.

However, *I* couldn't argue with *him* when he said if we interfered with others' free will, we showed we were no more evolved than they. Since the Universe expressed itself through free will, our task was to offer Earth's sentients a less fearful way of living, rather than forcing them into it. Therefore, the rehab chamber was out.

"Look at it this way, Rose. Awakening is a natural progression. For it to happen naturally, each must be allowed the time they as individuals require to Awaken naturally. With Earth, we are dictating the timetable. We all know why, but to me, it is still wrong to force them, to deny them a choice."

"They'll thank us later," I told him.

"More than likely, but it still feels wrong."

What could I say? He was right.

In the end, after consulting one more time with the Five, Bren and I decided our first move would be to return to the place where Linda had attacked Mac, and I'd been held. We planned to land right on top of their building, then force them to acknowledge our presence and face their fears, which we would then quickly transmute. If we Awakened them, Ian had assured us, then the Awakening would spread to all the other Misaligned Ones.

"Kind of like a virus?" I'd asked.

"Exactly," Ian replied. "We infect them with the Awakening, and those they are linked with will eventually Awaken as well."

"You are aware once they recover from the euphoria, they will invent all kinds of reasons to return to their old habits of thought, aren't you?" I asked Bren. "People used to having control and power are reluctant to give it up."

He smiled that special Bren smile at me, knowing how crazy I was about that damned dimple. "Then we'll take them on more and more trips, over and over again, for as long as it takes."

"Not a problem," I said, since leading folks on Indescribable Happy Tours was rapidly becoming one of my favorite pastimes.

We'd been giving a lot of Tours lately, and getting quite adept at knowing each individual or group's limitations. I did feel, though, there might be some truth to the idea of killing with kindness. If we weren't careful, Bren and I could fry people like the 9th had fried Bren during their first encounter. Unfortunately, there were only two sentients in the whole of creation who could survive *that* rendezvous.

"But what about those witnessing our arrival on the news and listening over the radio? How should we handle that?" I asked.

"Good question. Ian!" Bren called over his shoulder.

"Hmmmm?" Ian asked absently, most of his brain still engrossed in his algorithms about my sudden re-appearance.

"Got another puzzle for you to solve."

He lifted his head then. "Puzzle?" He grinned.

"What do we do with all the terrified people who will be watching TV and listening on the radio when we arrive?" I asked. "There are tons of horror movies about aliens invading from outer space and decimating humanity. It's one of our greatest fears."

"No doubt placed within your DNA eons ago by the Misaligned Ones," said Ian, dryly.

"It doesn't matter how the fear got there," Bren commented. "It's real, and the people of Earth need to be spared as much anxiety as possible."

He glanced at me and raised his brow. "What? You've got that look."

"What look?" I asked.

"The one that means you've just had an inspired idea."

"Well-l-l," I began, "now that you mention it, I do have a rather inspired idea. I just don't know if it will work."

"Well-l-l," Bren said, parroting me, "are you going to share it so we can make it work?"

I sat forward. "Okay, what if we make this first trip to Earth as covert as possible, focusing only on the Misaligned Ones and their Lairs?"

"Lairs?"

I shrugged, "I watched too many secret agent movies growing up." I waved my hand. "Anyway, we would be covert and, therefore, we could sidestep a lot of the initial fear factor."

I looked at Bren, then Ian, then back to Bren.

"Well? What do you think, gentlemen?"

The gentlemen smiled.

* * *

It had taken a long five weeks to get ready, although Bren had told me over and over this was the fastest campaign organization and implementation he had ever witnessed. If that was the case, then our Indescribable Happy journeys probably had a lot to do with it.

And, alas, I still hadn't managed to visit Astragon 7. But we would go, as soon as we had implemented Bren's plan to assist Earth's Awakening. In fact, as soon as we were convinced Earth was well on it's way to becoming a model citizen of the Collective, Bren and I were going to slip off into the sunset and live our own personal happily ever after.

But first things first.

The underground parking lot was full this time, and well lit, very different from the atmosphere surrounding Mac's almost-tragic rendezvous with Linda.

Bren and I teleported in behind a concrete pillar, and then he took off to scout the area.

"Only one guard at the door," he informed me.

"I guess that's where we will begin, then" I answered.

I maintained my watch, but heard the rustle of fabric when Bren returned to crouch beside me.

"Hi," I said. I really didn't need to speak, since we'd become so entangled we could read each other's thoughts almost before they reached our own consciousness. But I wanted him to look at me. I wanted to see the way his eyes sparkled when he saw me. I wanted to hear his deep, husky voice. See his dimple.

But of course he knew that.

"Hi," he replied, his love washing over me.

My stomach did its usual little flip-flop.

I closed my eyes and breathed it in. "Blessed are the peacemakers," I said.

"For they shall inherit the Earth," he replied.

"Shall we make some peace?" I asked. "Enter their Lair?"

We rose together, hands reaching out on their own, fingers clasping, as we stepped away from the shadows.

"Get down on your knees, hands behind your back! Now!" the armed guard at the entrance demanded as soon as he saw us.

But we had other plans. A thrill ran through me. "This is gonna to be fun," I whispered, fixing my attention on our welcoming committee of one.

Bren looked at me, grinning. "Ready?"

I nodded, and together we began to glow and expand, glow and expand, getting brighter and brighter, expanding further and further.

The guard gasped, and then a smile began to steal across his face.

"That's one," I thought.

Finis

Thoughts and bits of memories flitted randomly in and out of my consciousness; some of them his and some of them mine. It was the strangest feeling to think of my life as being the nighttime dreams of another. Just odd.

And, odder still, I had wound up where I had wound up; my body wasn't even the one I was born with, even though I couldn't tell any difference. Instead, it was some super-human indestructible thing made out of…what in the heck is Silistel?

Odd.

Creepy odd.

I didn't really want to think too long about that at the moment.

Instead, I studied the mem-unit's headset, turning it around and around. It was a band of silver metal which encircled the head. I had learned during my Bren-memory-immersion there were pressure points stimulating different parts of the brain when it was played back. When recording, those pressure points picked up information, providing very real, 3-D memories with all the sights, sounds, smells, tastes, thoughts and feelings as vivid as on the day they happened. All of which was stored in the little mem-unit—no bigger than an mp3 player—that was lying beside me.

I sighed, missing my own mp3 player. Music had always been my lifeline. I used it like a drug…to pull me out of moods, or to set moods, or just to carry me away when I wanted to imagine and write. I wondered if they had anything like that here. Something told me I'd need a bunch of happy tunes to lean on while I came to terms with this new life of mine.

Yep, I sure missed my music player.

Feeling eyes upon me, I glanced over at Bren. He was studying me, trying to read what I was feeling.

"Hi," I told him.

"Hello, Rose," he replied. There was relief when he spoke.

And something else I couldn't quite label. Concern? Responsibility? I couldn't guess.

"Was the mem-unit helpful?"

I gathered the two pieces together and glanced at them. "Very helpful. Thank you. Although…" I glanced at him and then away, "I 'm feeling like I invaded your privacy, and I apologize for that."

"I could not think of another way to help you with these changes," he replied, absently rubbing his beard. "I feared I had made a terrible mistake in bringing you here and putting you into that corpus." He did not look at me. Was he ashamed? "Because I didn't have your permission," he added, still scratching his beard.

"You saved my life, Brennar," I said. "It's too late to change things, and I'll adjust. I must adjust," I added.

"Yes," he said quietly.

"I think," I said slowly, "I'd like to be alone for a while."

Bren's disappointment washed over me in a wave of emotion. It was a physical thing. We were that connected to one another. I reached out and touched his hand, smiling. "It's nothing personal. I just need to be alone with my own thoughts."

He returned my smile and sighed, nodding. "I, of all people, understand. It's ...." His voice trailed off and he looked at me helplessly.

I am not an idiot. I knew the man was deeply in love with me. Not only that, he felt responsible for me, and he knew to his bones the turmoil I was going through. But he couldn't help me. He was one of the things I needed to work through.

I held up his mem-unit. "May I hold on to this? Go through it again?"

He smiled, relieved he could do something. "Of course, Rose."

The way he said my name flowed through me like liquid love. I shook my head, wanting to dive into his love, but also afraid of drowning, and quietly laughed at my reaction. I ran my hand through my hair, my fingers catching in the curls. "Thanks," I said, and waited for him to leave.

He fingered his beard again. "I should shave my beard. It's against regulations," he mused. "May I come back later and check on you?"

"Of course, Brennar," I replied, politely. 5ths appeared to be a very polite group.

He literally brightened as he rose to leave, his eyes never leaving my face.

After he left, I sat for several minutes staring at the door.

I could never have imagined the depth one could be loved. It was a little unnerving.

Did I love him in return, as deeply? My body sure did,

and not just in a sexual manner. The DNA we share thrilled at his presence. But that was my body's reaction, and I had no idea what my own was. This new, unknown body was something that was pieced together from bits of me, and bits of something else. It wasn't really the body I knew anymore.

And he and I were so hopelessly entangled I didn't know my own thoughts anymore, either. All this time. All those novels I had written! They weren't from my vivid imagination. They were from him. Borrowed memories of his missions. I looked down at the mem-unit containing Bren's latest experiences. It was frightening how my latest novel's outline mirrored what I'd just learned.

I sighed.

Did I even know who I was anymore? I certainly didn't feel very real right now. In fact, it felt like it would be very easy to slip into madness. I shivered and shook my head, forcing myself to think other thoughts. "It is what it is," I whispered. "Deal, Malone." I clung to the fact my voice sounded like me.

I looked again at the mem-unit, studying its settings. From Bren's memories, I had noticed the settings were at a frequency setting a little higher than an average 3rd. Nice to think Bren felt I was above average in that department. On a whim, I changed the frequency to a 5th, fitted the headset back on my head and settled back to experience Bren's memories from his point of view.

There are no words to describe the difference between viewing those memories as a 3rd and then seeing them again as a 5th. The gulf between those two realities was almost insurmountable, like seeing two completely different stories. Or, rather, two completely different perspectives: one from a child's perspective and one from a wise adult.

I'm not saying either perspective was wrong. A child brings newness and delight. An adult brings maturity and experience. It was just intensely different.

I remember standing on the summit of a mountain peak, some 14,000 feet up. Everything looked more intense and clear. The sky and small flowers were so very vivid. The air was crisper and smelled clean and pure. The sun burned with more heat upon my shoulders. The sound of a marmot's high cry carried so much further. And I could see for miles off into the blue haze as the Earth curved into infinity. It was all just so much *more*.

That was how I felt, reviewing Bren's memories from a 5th's perspective. And when I got to the approach to Astragon 7, its beauty so overwhelmed me I had tears streaming down my face and was forced to turn off the unit.

I had never seen anything as beautiful in my life as that space station. I had to see it for myself. I had to make some of Bren's memories my own so I could differentiate and find myself again.

I felt so lost.

So very lost, like the book title *A Stranger in a Strange Land*. I was definitely in a strange land, but I was also in a strange body.

I couldn't help myself. I needed to see more of Astragon 7, and so I flipped the mem-unit back on.

He found me that way, sitting helplessly, weeping at the beauty of what his memories showed me. I blindly reached out for him and he gathered me close.

"Take me there." I whispered, my voice choked with

tears.

"Where?" he asked, as he gently disengaged me from the mem-unit, setting it aside.

I reached out and touched his face…his beardless face…sharing with him what I had been watching.

And he got it! From my touch, he not only understood where I wanted to go, but why.

I felt my eyes widen. I pulled back a little to look at him. "I didn't know we could communicate like that."

Bren grinned. "I didn't, either," he said. He reached out and carefully wiped the tears from my eyes with the corner of the bed sheet. "We are a twisted mess, are we not?" he said softly. "But have faith, Rose. We will sort this through. You'll see."

I sighed and leaned against his warmth, soaking up his strength, and surrendering to a safe, enfolding intimacy that felt like what Bren had described in the mem-unit as Touch. No wonder his heart had hurt when he thought it was gone.

* * *

Unfortunately, the feeling did not last. A couple of days later, although feeling a little less fragile, I was restless and claustrophobic. Bren found me pacing my room, counting my footsteps out loud. My body's reflexes and responses were so fast, my timing was totally off. Add that to its extreme sensitivity and I was a shambles. I felt like a colt learning to walk, or Bambi on ice.

I stopped my pacing, turned and looked at Bren. "I need a gym," I announced, hands on my hips.

He cocked his head at me, one eyebrow raised.

"I need to *move*, Bren! I'm feeling…" I paused, searching for the words, "…caged and clumsy. I want to move and get used to this body and-and get *out* of this room!"

He nodded slowly, his face clouding. "I agree, being active in your corpus will help you adapt to it. However, to all but a few, you don't exist. I don't think it's a good idea for you to be seen until we can create proper identification and a reason for being on Sal 5."

I growled in frustration. "You don't understand, Bren. I really, really need to move. It's what I do when I'm overloaded with emotions. Please?" I begged, thinking surely he was sensitive enough to feel the emotions simmering under the surface, emotions barely contained. "I really need to do something familiar." I added, fisting my hands in my hair. "I feel like I'm losing my mind, here."

I reached out and grabbed his hand so he could feel all the emotions roiling within me.

I was having a very bad day.

Bren found me a gym.

I followed him through a maze of corridors and modules until we reached a large open space with partitions on one side. I probably could have followed my nose and found it. It smelled like a gym, apparently a universal scent.

The gym wasn't very crowded, just a few people working out at some equipment and a couple more playing some hand and ball game, sort of a basketball without a basket. The squeak of their shoes echoed against the high ceiling and bulkheads. The partitions looked like large, square stalls whose walls stopped about halfway to the high ceiling, with doors to provide a semblance of privacy. Some of the doors were closed, and I heard voices, grunts, and thumps coming from behind them. The floors of the open stalls were matted, so I assumed they were used to practice hand-to-hand combat and the like. In the last partitioned stall hung a punching bag, suspended from the ceiling.

Also suspended from the ceiling was a track. Craning my neck, I could see only one or two people using it. I'd be virtually alone.

"Perfect," I told Bren. "How do I get up there?"

He led me to a ladder that looked like something a trapeze artist would use.

"Seriously?" I asked.

He grinned, "If you're using the gym on Sal 5, then you're training. It's just another exercise, and a good warm-up for track use." He gestured for me to climb.

I made a face. "I think it's a way for people to secretly check out each other's bottoms," I said as I grabbed the rungs and began to climb.

The ladder shifted when Bren began to follow. "Ummm, Bren?" I looked down at him as the rope ladder swayed under our combined weight. "I'm still feeling awkward in this new body and I want to do this alone for now, do you mind?"

He looked at me blankly.

"I'm clumsy and self-conscious. I don't really want an audience." I told him bluntly, making a wry face. "It won't be a pretty sight."

"Ah," he said with an understanding nod and climbed back down. "Shall I come back in about an hour?"

"Perfect. Thanks," I said.

"An hour, then." He turned with a smile and headed toward the entrance.

I watched him go, thinking how beautifully he moved. Not one wasted movement, like a cat, a cat with rippling muscles. I used to be able to move like that. I wanted to again. Soon.

At the top of the ladder, I hoisted myself onto a platform that ringed the track, did a couple of stretches and walked onto the springy surface. It was four lanes wide and I selected the outer one. My first few steps were so poorly executed I swore with frustration. All the muscle memory from thousands of martial arts practices, thousands of runs on the beach, thousands of bike rides and other activities, had been instilled in a different body. Whose it had been and where it was now, I'd rather not think about.

Taking a deep breath, I calmed my mind and thought back to what I remembered from the mem-unit regarding Bren's adjustment to his Silistel corpus. It was gratifying to know the man who now moved like a cat had had similar struggles. But the new body thing wasn't an issue for him in concept, since he'd had so many. I'd only had one, and I was missing my old one. A lot.

Since those thoughts weren't helping me any, I shook my head to clear them and refocused on the task at hand.

I took a couple of slow-motion practice jogs around the track. By the third circuit, my body had caught on and I hit my stride. Heartened, I did a series of starts, stops, short sprints and then settled into a nice pace for a long run.

My new body was a very fast learner. I felt myself

grinning with satisfaction and I relaxed, enjoying the view. Below, I could see other people going through their workout routines. Then, I tuned everything else out and just ran, feeling how my new muscles cooperated with one another like a beautifully precisioned machine. What had Bren called it? The difference between a star fighter and a freighter? Oh, yeahhhh…

I don't know how long I ran, but I felt stronger and stronger as I went along, not the outcome I was looking for. I wanted to be so tired I wouldn't be able to think for a while. Since that plan wasn't working, and since I was feeling like SuperGirl, I pushed my body, deciding to ascertain its limits. Faster and faster I raced around the track, reveling in it. It felt great to move, to get rid of the frustration and confusion by applying myself to something I could do well.

I was so focused within it took me a while to notice the pounding footfalls coming up from behind me. When a strong hand landed on my shoulder, I immediately dropped and spun, sweeping my leg and tripping my assailant.

Only it wasn't an assailant.

It was Bren.

"Oh, my God!" I kneeled beside him, "I'm so sorry! Are you okay?"

For a moment we were silent as we regained our breath.

In the silence, I realized no one below us was active anymore. Instead, they were all gazing up…at us. I could tell by Bren's expression he wasn't too happy with me. To the majority of those on the Salinio 5, I didn't exist. And they certainly didn't know my body was the same kind of Silistel corpus as his.

"What's going on?" I whispered to Bren as he pulled me to my feet.

He glanced at me and grinned slightly. "You were faster than humanly possible."

I clapped my hand over my mouth.

He nodded towards the ladder. "We have exactly as long as it takes to get down from this platform to devise an explanation."

"Oh, God," I groaned. "I am so sorry, Bren." I could feel my face heating as I frantically tried to think of some reason I could have been running so fast.

"Are those the prototype trainers I've been reading about?" a voice from below asked as we were nearing the end of our descent.

I looked down, surprised, and even more so once I spotted the imp of a girl who was at least four inches shorter than me. She grinned, her eyes twinkling. "How do you and your people always manage to get the new gizmos, Bren?" she asked putting out a hand to steady me as she lifted my foot for inspection. "They don't look that special," she commented.

"They aren't meant to," Bren replied and turned towards me. "How did you enjoy them?"

He looked at me, expectantly.

"I didn't," I said emphatically. "I totally lost control."

I looked at the woman who was still holding my foot. "Didn't you see us crash?"

The Pixie, for I now recognized her from Bren's mem-

251

unit as Captain Frankie Pritican, grinned at me, finally releasing my foot. "I did see that," she said. "In fact, we all saw it. In fact, I doubt any of us will be lining up to purchase these trainers any time soon."

"And we will not be recommending them," Bren said dryly.

That brought a chuckle from some of those who were still within earshot, our audience having rapidly lost interest and now returning to what they'd been doing before.

Frankie Pritican glanced at the digital readout of the time on the gym's wall. "I do believe we have a couple of hours before dinner time. Why don't I show this brave volunteer the locker rooms, so she can clean up...and then I can take her for a well-deserved drink. Okay with you?" she asked Bren. "We will take good care of the shoes, although I doubt anyone wants to try them now they've seen what they can do."

I looked helplessly at Bren when the petite Pixie grabbed my hand in a grip much stronger than I'd anticipated and towed me into the woman's locker room.

He grinned and waved me on.

The minute we stepped into the room and Frankie confirmed we were alone, she burst into peals of laughter. "I love to see that expression on Bren's face." she told me. "And I'll never let him forget how I saved his skin yet again."

I followed her to where she had stored her duffle. She pulled it out and kept talking as she rummaged through it. "I'm Frankie Pritican, by the way, and I obviously know who you are, Anna Rose Malone." She glanced at me briefly. "And what you are." She grinned again, and let out another peal of laughter. "You should have seen everyone below, with their mouths hanging open watching you run faster and faster until you were a blur."

I gaped at her. "I was a blur?"

She nodded. "A definite blur."

"Wow. No wonder Bren looked so…uh….concerned after he stopped me."

She laughed again. "From where I was standing, it looked like you stopped Bren."

I smiled. "Well, he took me by surprise. I just reacted without thinking." I paused, realizing I was feeling more comfortable in my skin. "Thanks, by the way. That was quick thinking. Bren," I shook my head, "he really doesn't want people to know about me yet."

"At least not what you are," she replied, nodding in agreement. "But that doesn't mean you can't be seen out having a little fun. Here," she said, shoving some fatigues into my hands. "You can use these. Let's get showered and then go to the pub and get acquainted."

Twenty minutes later, I was sitting across from her in the corner of a little bar two levels above the gym. Finding it impossible to decipher the menu, I glanced up to see Frankie watching me.

I flung the menu down and threw my hands up. "I've no idea what this menu says," I told her. "I can't read it."

"Not a problem," she answered with a smile. "Does all this frustrate you?"

I shrugged. "A bit," I replied, not trying to hide the sarcasm.

Her dark eyes filled with compassion. "I can't imagine how strange this all must seem to you," she said waving her hand to encompass our surroundings and nodding at the window with its view of Montorea.

"A bit," I said again, smiling slightly.

"Sometimes having a friendly ear helps," she said, cocking her head. "Mine may be pointy, but it hears just fine."

I took a breath and let it out slowly. "That is a lovely offer, thank you." I told her. "But what would help me more is to tell me a little bit about yourself. Just so I can focus on something other than me and my predicament."

"Sure," she said warmly.

A little robot that looked like a floating tray arrived soundlessly to take our order.

"Two Resusses," she told it.

It beeped and repeated the order in a mechanical voice and floated off toward the bar. A couple of minutes later, it returned carrying two drinks. Frankie handed both to me and held her identification bracelet up for scanning, but the robot beeped again. "The two officers at the bar have paid for your beverages," it told us.

The Pixie glanced over her shoulder and gave them a friendly yet uninviting wave of thanks. They grinned and lifted their chins in acknowledgment.

I smiled, thinking of my editor, Lacy. It was a bittersweet memory, and I banked down the pang and re-focused on the moment.

I handed Frankie her drink and we saluted each other with our glasses.

I took a tentative sip and sighed contentedly, as I felt the icy liquid go down my throat. "This is good," I told her. "It reminds me of a drink back on Earth called a Lemon Drop. Very refreshing."

I took another sip and smiled at her.

She returned my smile. "This is my favorite drink. Glad you like it. But I warn you, you may not want to have too many if you plan to stay on your feet," she giggled, taking another sip. "Why don't I tell you a story of my cadet days?" she offered. "I'll think of one that includes Brennar."

I leaned forward, ready for what could only be a tall tale. "I suspect anything you have to tell me about Brennar Faulkner would not have shown up on his mem-unit."

I smiled at Frankie, liking her. A lot. She bubbled with contagious enthusiasm, making it hard for me to be morose.

"Indeed not!" she chortled, tossing her head, the tips of her pointed ears peeking through her short blond hair. She scrunched up her face. "I wonder which story I should tell you?" she mused, tapping her lip. "Okay, I've got it," she said, snapping her fingers after a short silence. Taking another sip from her drink she settled back into her chair with a half smile.

But before she got started, the little floating droid returned with a light flashing.

Frankie glanced at me. "Message light," she told me, and pushed the indicator. It was a messages from the two men who had bought our drinks telling us they were leaving, but if we "two cute ladies" would like to meet them at a later date, to tell the droid.

"Do you get tired of being told how cute you are?" I

asked her after Frankie very politely thanked them and said the two cute ladies were spoken for.

She sighed and nodded. "I'm the Perky Pixie. Doesn't matter I can fly circles around most other pilots." She nodded toward the jacket hanging on the back of her chair. "It helps some when they know I outrank them, but without my jacket on, I could be any rank."

I nodded in understanding. "My nickname on Earth was 'Angel with a Pen.'" I rolled my eyes. "It sold books, though. Otherwise, I would have hated it. I'm not saying I don't like the way I look. I just don't appreciate it when a man decides who I am based only on my looks. I think that's one reason why I like being an author. I don't have to look any particular way. I just have to be good at it."

She raised her glass to me. "To cute, perky Pixies and speedy angels."

I clinked mine with her, adding, "And to tiny but strong women everywhere."

Together, we tipped back our heads and finished our drinks. My new perky Pixie friend ordered another round that was paid for by yet another group of young cadets who gazed at us hopefully. This time I thanked them and gently let them know we weren't interested. We touched glasses again and Frankie began her story.

"Most of the people you see here are cadets or those awaiting new orders, since Sal 5 is the Keepers' headquarters. Cadets come here to be trained and, if they pass, they're accepted into the Corps' ranks," she began.

"Like boot camp...no, wait, more like what I learned about training for what's called special forces on Earth," I said. "You are trained and tested, but if you don't make the grade or you don't like it, you're assigned elsewhere."

"Exactly," she said. "I always wanted to be a pilot, but I couldn't afford the commercial cost of pilot school, so I enlisted," she continued. "Met Bren the first day when we were all lined up in Assembly." She smiled, her eyes far away. "We were packed in shoulder to shoulder. Could barely move, and I, being so short, could not see a darn thing," she winked, "except for lots of great-looking posteriors."

I laughed.

"Bren happened to be standing beside me," Frankie continued. "When he noticed my problem, he began describing what was going on. Only, he made it so funny I had a very hard time keeping a straight face. He kept comparing the speakers to different creatures, and some were not so complimentary."

I laughed, seeing a more playful side to Bren than I had imagined, and I told Frankie as much.

"He was very playful at first. He got more serious as he earned more responsibility. But I can still see his playful side at certain moments. Mac keeps Brennar playful. I am very glad Mac is his Second."

I nodded, grinning to myself about Mac and his expletive collection.

"As a cadet," Frankie continued, "Bren first displayed his leadership skills by organizing harmless pranks. Things like changing the locks on cadets' doors, or switching duties so one person would keep getting the same nasty or smelly task." She smirked. "I kept getting assigned to making the drill sergeant's bunk, and I always got marks against me because I can't seem to ever make a tidy bed." She shook her head. "Another was module storage. After so many months, we cadets would be sent on short practice missions, and our belongings would be stored in modules until we returned. Brennar and I somehow managed to reassign a couple of the modules into long-term storage." She laughed. "And while Bren was setting it up, I snuck his module number into the group we had designated for long-term storage, not knowing he was doing the exact same thing to me!"

I laughed. "So you pranked each other."

She nodded, giggling. "But here's the best prank, although it had some serious ramifications, so take it as a cautionary tale." She took a sip of her Resus cocktail. "One of the cadets who entered the program with us, Regulus was his name, was not appropriate for the Corps. We all sensed it immediately." She paused. "How can I describe him without being negative about it?" She shrugged. "Unfortunately, I can't," she told me ruefully. "So I won't, and hope you will not think less of me."

She took a breath.

"The best way to describe Regulus is to call him a Border 5th, leaning more toward a 3rd than a 5th." She grimaced, "Sorry, because I know that's where people who know about you have slotted you so they can come to terms with who you are. But I don't think you and Regulus are alike at all. He was very inappropriate as a Keeper candidate. He wanted to be a Keeper solely because he loved being able to command and control people. He was not the least interested in guiding Awakenings." She shrugged. "That's the best I can do to describe his character."

I nodded. "There are people like that out there," I said.

"Not all 3rds are the same, and I figure not all 5ths are, either."

"Exactly." Frankie said. "Anyway, during our probation period, each cadet takes on the leadership role of their platoon for two months. When your turn comes, you move out of group quarters and into a single and larger suite or rooms; all part of the psychology of being a leader. The leadership role is the tipping point. How well one does during their two months as leader determines their whole Keeper career. Our names are posted, so it is no surprise when each cadet's two months happen. What was a surprise was the instant Regulus's period began, a huge container ship…did I mention his family owned a shipping business, one of the largest in galaxy? "

I shook my head, relaxing into the story and the alcohol, waiting to hear more.

"So this ship arrives," Frankie said, "carrying a whole new set of furnishings for Regulus's new quarters." She shook her head. "Unheard of. But, obviously Regulus's parents knew people high up within the Keepers, and it was allowed, because crewmembers from the container ship brought the furnishings to Regulus and set them up for him. The prize item was an exquisite, handmade cabinet for one's alcoholic beverages."

"A liquor cabinet?" I asked, holding up my glass.

She nodded. "A liquor cabinet. Its inside was carved so the necks of the liquor bottles slipped into especially made slots, and then the bottle bottoms rested on shelves below. And for the first month, at the end of each week, Regulus would hold a party for those under his leadership who had served him best. Of course they were always the same people, and of course they were his cronies. And of course it was entirely unfair and created dissension. And…" she paused, "…Bren decided it was a perfect opportunity for a prank."

Another droid came over with two more drinks, gifted to us by yet more flirtatious cadets. We were both so caught up in the story we barely acknowledged their enthusiastic waves. Finishing the last of drinks number two, we set the empty glasses on the droid's tray.

"Dirtside on Montorea are some rather nasty night fliers called Kerilacs. They sleep during the day in dark caves and, if disturbed, they set up an awful squawking while loudly emitting a noxious odor from their bottoms." She grimaced and shuddered. "The odor lingers. Clings to clothing, skin, furnishings…everything."

I could feel my eyebrows lifting high. "Tell me you did not put those things in the liquor cabinet."

She began to twinkle. "Kerilacs have lovely, long necks that fit beautifully where a bottle neck would be."

"Alive?"

"Yes, of course alive. Otherwise, it wouldn't have been the perfect prank."

"How?"

Frankie leaned forward on her elbows in a conspiratorial manner. I caught myself mimicking her. "Bren had thought it all out. He found a means to bring eight Kerilacs from Montorea via medical dispatch, explaining they were needed for a practice mission. The beasties arrived, packaged neatly in an artificial sleep container. He had also arranged for Regulus to be gone from his quarters to a meeting—with an Admiral, no less. While Regulus was gone, we sneaked into his quarters, unpacked his liquor cabinet and repacked it with the sleeping Kerilacs, all hanging neatly in a row with their long necks extended." She giggled. "And then we waited for the night's party."

"What happened?" I asked eagerly.

"Well, things went slightly awry," she told me. "What Bren had not known was the Admiral he had arranged to meet with Regulus just happened to be an old friend of Regulus's father and the whole reason both Regulus and his liquor cabinet were on Sal 5 in the first place. So, when the liquor cabinet was opened for that night's festivities..." she smiled slowly. "Let's just say both Regulus and the Admiral had front row seats."

"Oh no," I said with a huge grin. "Poetic justice."

She giggled, hands over her mouth. "It was spectacular! I've never seen a room clear out so fast in my life!"

"But the aftermath?"

"Equally spectacular, but not nearly as funny. If it hadn't been for Bren taking the full brunt of the punishment and never naming names, I would never have been able to become a pilot. And if it weren't for Bren's brother and the people he knew in the Watchers Division, Bren would have been discharged immediately." She smiled. "But that didn't happen, and I choose instead to remember Regulus's expression when he learned his prized cabinet was to be used to transport the Kerilacs back to their cave on Montorea. You see, nobody wanted to risk opening the thing again once it was closed."

I laughed.

"As far as I know," she said, "it's still there, a roost for

Kerilacs!"

Our conversation drifted to other topics, until we finished our drinks and thought it best to leave while we could still a) walk and b) find Bren's quarters.

Wending my way through the maze of modules, I wondered if I'd ever find the pub again without Frankie's help and I said as much.

"Not to worry, Rose. I'll take you back there any time."

"Thank you, Frankie, for your company," I said, enunciating very carefully, when we arrived at Bren's room panel. "I needed it."

She smiled and touched my hand. "When we first arrive at a planet under cover, we all feel a little unsettled. I imagine you feel that tenfold. I'm glad I could give you ease." She grinned suddenly. "And I was curious about the woman who has captured Bren's heart."

That was how I learned this new corpus did more than just blush. It also glowed.

Chapter 21- Meeting the League of Five

It was very strange meeting people for the very first time, but who I had intimate knowledge of because of Bren's mem-unit. All very déjà vu. I was so glad that, aside from Frankie Pritican's Pixieness, they all looked pretty human. From the mem-unit I had learned that the known universe was mostly populated by human-type folk the Keepers called sentients. But I wasn't quite ready to meet the others, especially the blue one. Who was that? Carringdon?

The League of Five sat in a circle around a small table in the corner of my little room. It was really too small for all of us. We were nearly sitting shoulder-to-shoulder and knee-to-knee, which seemed to increase my feelings of unease.

Bren sat to my right, and I reached for his hand, at the same time wishing I felt more independent. Even with my new friendship with Frankie, I wasn't nearly settled into my situation. It'd only been a couple of weeks since I had arrived here in this science fiction world.

This was the third room I'd been moved to. The first room was a lot like a hospital room, because Doc still wanted to monitor my assimilation into this new body of mine. The second room was in a rehab wing of the space station. They moved me there for a couple of days to make sure all my working parts were…working.

This third room reminded me of a comfortable but no-frills hotel room. It could be anywhere in the world and, truth be told, I did pretend for a bit it was. But my fantasy, such as it was, didn't last very long. All I had to do was look out through the thick, sealed window and see a planet not unlike Earth circling below me. It was a pretty sight, but where were North America, Europe or China? All the continents were different shapes from the ones I'd had drilled into me during grade school geography lessons.

Disconcerting.

The best part about the room was it was right next door to Bren's, and that was a huge relief, for Brennar Faulkner had become my safety net. I'd written so much about him in my novels, I'd shared his memories, and then there was this hybrid thing we shared. He was the only person who really understood what I was going through. Thank God he'd had the foresight to put that mem-unit on my head when he did. I really do feel I had been on the brink of madness at that point. And, if I'm being honest with myself, I think I'm still not too far away from it.

But it comes in waves. When I'm curious, I can handle things. Have always been that way.

Bren and I had discussed when we could go to Astragon 7. He felt we should start with something more like what I had been used to and suggested we go his cabin on Montorea. There, I would have the familiar experience of being on a planet, and we would have the freedom to learn more about our Silistel bodies far away from the scrutiny of others.

The other option was to stay with Bren's brother, Ian, and be surrounded by Domena's harmonics. But I wasn't ready for more strangers. I'd rather hide in the woods.

It was best, if possible, to experience one thing at a time to avoid becoming overwhelmed. My outing at the gym and subsequent talk with Frankie, although fun, had been overwhelming, and had taken me a couple of days to assimilate. I think it was the parallels to my life on Earth that did it to me.

I wanted to leave for that cabin immediately.

But, first things first: the League of Five.

Not surprisingly, the last thing I wanted to be doing at the moment was sitting crammed around a tiny table nearly touching knees with all Five of the League. I really wanted to bolt and get started learning about myself

Although Bren was the leader of the group, it was the Guardian guy, Langsford, who broke the awkward silence, just as I was beginning to wonder if the meeting was going to take place telepathically. You never knew about aliens.

"How are you faring, Annarosemalone?" he asked, his dark eyes searching my face.

"You don't have to use my whole name. Rose will do," I explained. "Or Rosie or M,'" I added as an afterthought.

"Which do you prefer?" Langsford asked.

I shrugged. "Rose is fine," I said.

He nodded. "This must be a difficult experience for you," he ventured. "How are you faring?"

I shot a glance at Bren. "Business as usual," I answered.

Bren smiled.

"That is how I tried to handle my adjustment to this new corpus." Bren explained to the others. "I focused on the tasks at hand, my PeaceKeepers' responsibilities."

I nodded. "What else can I do?" I asked, releasing Bren's hand and wrapping my arms tight around myself. "I have my life, and I am very grateful for that. I know it will take time for me to adjust. How long? That I do not know."

Frankie Pritican caught my eye and gave me a small, encouraging smile. She was such a tiny thing! It was hard to think of her as a soldier. I knew my answering smile was a bit tremulous, but I winked at her, letting her know I was grateful for our new friendship.

"We apologize for interrupting your recovery and adjustment period," Langsford said, "but it would be most helpful if you would tell us how you were captured."

I tightened my arms around myself even more. "I don't feel ready to talk about it," I told him. "Besides, I don't remember much of that time."

"But you will try?" he asked gently. "Even a little information from you is more than we have today."

I reached for Bren's hand again and took a breath, nodding. "Okay. Yes, I will try."

Ian, Brennar's brother, leaned forward. "What if she used a mem-unit? Perhaps it will give her relief." Like Bren, he was a strikingly handsome man. In their own way, each man in that room was strikingly handsome. Pretty people, these 5ths.

"I feel she needs to be Witnessed, Ian," Bren answered. He squeezed my hand, "If we hear her story, she can heal more cleanly."

Ian sat back, nodding. "Perhaps so."

"Whenever you are ready, Rose," Bren said.

The energy that came from his hand flowed with warmth and reminded me the past really was history.

Never one to procrastinate for long, I took a deep breath and began.

"I met a man," I said, "And we felt an instant attraction to one another, or so I believed." I laughed a little. "I've been so busy writing I really did not have time to meet new people. But Lacy, my editor, came up with this great publicity stunt. She held a Joss Walker Look-Alike Contest. She had my fans send in pictures of people they knew who looked like my character. The ones who most looked like Joss Walker would be invited to the Romantic Times Convention, and I would select the winner.

I paused, acutely missing Lacy, swallowed it down, and continued with a sigh.

"That's where I met Sam. He was one of the finalists. And he was a fan of my books. It was quite an ego boost to meet a man who had actually read my novels. Granted, they were science fiction romance novels written for entertainment, but I take my writing very seriously and do as much research as possible." I smiled at the memory. "To find someone as fascinated as I was with the world I had created! And an intelligent, handsome man who I actually liked! It was a dream come true for me. We would even hash out storylines together. He was a physicist and a science fiction fan. He could tell me if I had any scientific support for the ideas springing into my head while I wrote or outlined my next novel. It was great, you see, because I was contracted to write two books a year. That didn't give me much time to play. But with Sam I was working and playing."

I paused, squeezing my eyes shut. I was getting to the ugly stuff. I took a deep breath, trying to slow down my breathing. "That happy time with Sam lasted about four and a half months." I took another breath and unclenched my jaw. "In an instant, it all changed."

I stopped speaking.

"It's over, Rose," Bren said gently. "You are safe now."

I nodded and swallowed.

"Would you like a few minutes?" Frankie asked, tucking her blond hair behind her pointy ears.

I glanced at her and smiled gratefully but shook my head. "No, I may as well get this over with. There's not much left to tell, anyway."

Bren's thumb brushed over the back of my hand. Good thing he was like me. Otherwise, I would have crushed his hand by now.

I relaxed my grip.

"One night," I continued, "while we were dining at a local restaurant, Sam must have put something in my wine, because suddenly, I had no control over anything. I could barely think, and I started slurring my words, and the room was spinning.

"From then on, everything gets all scrambled in my head. I remember he half-carried me out of the restaurant and there was a car waiting for us. The car was dark with darkened windows. Someone else helped me into the car. Another person congratulated Sam." I shrugged. "And that was the last I ever saw of him," I said.

"I've no idea how long I was in the car, but I must have fallen asleep. The next thing I remember is being physically hauled out of the car and carried into some hospital-type place. I was really out of it by then. I just remember voices and bright lights and those sanitized smells you get in places like that. I remember thinking I should be terrified and I wasn't, and that's what terrified me—which I didn't care what was going on. And then I went to sleep again.

"Next time I woke up, I was strapped to a hospital bed surrounded with drip bags filled with God knows what. I know people were asking me questions about my stories, and I remember mumbling back answers, so there must have been some sort of truth serum in those drip bag cocktails. They kept me like that for days. Who knows for how long? I just felt weaker and weaker, and I knew I would eventually die, although I didn't really care." I paused, thinking back. "I take that back. Actually, I really did care. I wanted to escape and if the only way to escape was to die, well then…fine by me."

I took a deep breath, letting it out slowly, and leaned back into my seat. "And then the next thing I remember was waking up here and seeing my fictitious character, Joss Walker."

I looked at Bren, my tone expressionless.

"Only it wasn't Joss. It was Brennar, and he had a beard." I shrugged, looking down at Bren's and my linked hands. "That's about it. I'm not sure how any of this will help you."

It was silent for several moments. After a while, I looked up to see identical expressions on each their faces.

* * *

I couldn't help it.

I burst out laughing.

The look of concerned sympathy on these hunky, beefcake men just cracked me up. A woman's fantasy come true—manly men with deep feelings, and not afraid to show them.

I looked at Mac.

"Fuck." I told him.

He blinked.

"Shit! Damn It! Son of a bitch! Mother Fucker! Asshole!"

He cocked his head.

"Expletives, Mac. From Earth. Here's another one. SNAFU. It's a military acronym and means 'Situation Normal, All Fucked Up'."

Mac looked at Bren who grinned at him. "Well, she has been plugged into my mem-unit, Mac," he reminded him.

"Yup," I glanced at Bren, and then turned back to my audience. "And it saved my sanity," I told them. "Although I still feel I'm on shaky ground, and I need a lot of time to process all …" I waved my hands around the room, "this weirdness. But I will," I assured them. "I will get through this. I am a survivor."

I glanced at Bren again. "I understand why you had the Doc, here, make me into a hybrid. I would not have wanted to be the only one in the Universe, either." He nodded and I smiled at the relief in his eyes. "But we have a lot to discover about what exactly we are. And I think working to understand all of this will help me adjust the fastest."

I glanced about the room. They still had that look.

"Honestly," I told them, "I *am* feeling okay at the moment. I think telling you what happened—the Witnessing-- has helped me. You can all relax a little." I turned to Bren. "Bren, tell them."

He nodded. "In truth, she has no distress. However, I feel it's necessary to take her to my cabin, especially since that's what she wants. She can have much-needed quiet, and we can learn more about our corpuses."

Langsford nodded. "Understood and agreed. However, we still must gain control over the situation on Earth. Our investigations will have to continue."

"Of course," said Bren. "And I can easily be present for all meetings."

"Bren?" Ian said. "After having Witnessed Rose's story, I would like to encourage her to stay with me and my family for a while before you take her to the cabin."

I shook my head and began to protest, but he interrupted.

"Please, Rose, let me explain my reasoning before you decline."

He waited for me to nod before he continued. "I have been doing extensive study of Earth, as you are aware. Aside from our advanced technologies, my home life is very similar to a middle class family on Earth. Our boys go to school, Domena is preparing to teach at the local university, and I have a government research job. We work, we play, we have family outings.

"I believe you would find how we live very soothing, Rose, because of these commonalities. And then there is my bondmate, Domena. She is a Harmonist—an artist as you are, in addition to being a healer and counselor. And, like you, she has just arrived on Montorea and has yet to meet other women. We would both very much like for you to stay with us for a few days. I do believe, with Domena's artistry, it would help you adjust."

I was quiet for a few moments, thinking about Ian's offer. Perhaps a non-military setting would help me. I remembered Bren's memories of his family visit, and it did feel fairly normal to me. Plus, they were living on a planet, one that was very similar to Earth.

I glanced at Bren.

"What do you think?" I asked. "Could we postpone the cabin visit for a few days?"

He barely hesitated before answering. "I believe that would be an excellent choice for you, Rose. I know they would take excellent care of you, and I believe you will like Domena very much. "

"And you could focus on the League," exclaimed Langsford, bringing the group back into focus.

"Indeed," agreed Bren. "And here's what I think we should do next…"

And with that, my situation was resolved and the League of Five meeting began in earnest.

I actually found myself enjoying their meeting. It was like being thrown into the middle of one of my novels, and so much better than a 3D movie. Much like my fictionalized Bren, he was a quiet leader who invited comments and opinions from those in the group, while still remaining in control. He listened to each of their reports, asked a series of questions and then formulated what he wanted to know by the next meeting, and what further actions should be taken in the meantime.

"If Rose agrees, I think it is time for her to download her memories into a mem-unit so you can study them," he told Ian. "It will help us understand the levels of paranoia we are dealing with. Plus, her subconscious should have recorded events her drugged mind could not recall. Perhaps we can glean more information from there as well." He looked at me. "Rose? Are you willing now to record those recent memories?"

I nodded. "It seems I should. I'm curious to see what you all can learn from it."

"Thank you, Rose," said Langsford.

I smiled at him. He had kind eyes. It was a little odd to think how mistrustful he was towards Bren. But that was Bren's opinion. I liked to form my own opinions, separate from the ones I had picked up from him.

"Mac," Bren continued, "once you have filtered through Rose's memories, ask Linda if she can provide any additional information about where Rose was taken. I will also download what I experienced when I collected Rose. Then when we have completed our downloads, I'll take her to Ian's house." He smiled and looked at each member of the group. "Any questions?"

There were none, so they discussed when they would be ready for the next meeting. After that was set, we rose and said our good-byes.

Before she left, I thanked Frankie again for saving me from the gym incident, for the drinks and stories at the pub, and for the clothes she'd loaned me.

She brightened, saying, "Always glad to find someone my size to share clothes with. It doesn't happen often. The wee folk must stick together."

I laughed, appreciating her cheerful spunkiness. "Yes, the wee and the mighty! Next time, I'll buy the drinks," I promised her.

She twinkled at me. "As long as we go into a bar alone together, I doubt either one of us will ever need to buy drinks."

We both giggled when Bren shot us a look.

Of all of them, Frankie was the one who most treated me as if I were one of them. I needed that.

The door to my room swished closed and I turned to face Bren, and caught him giving me one of those looks I chose not to think about. I shook my head to refocus my thoughts before I began to glow. "Now, how do we download my memories?" I asked.

"Follow me," he said.

Bren led me over to the room's standard issue desk, which consisted of a flat screen with various buttons and jacks, and gestured for me to sit. Pulling over a chair from the ones circling the little table, he sat beside me. "We won't use my personal unit, but rather the one anyone on Sal 5 can access. The League has its own code-protected section. It's where we file our reports and any other pertinent information. In fact, I'd like it if you take a look at it. Being a 3rd of Earth, I would welcome your insights and involvement. You could contribute a lot if you want to be involved."

I nodded. "I do want to be involved, thanks. It helps me, this keeping busy and staying in the present. Like I said, if I can keep curious and in problem-solving mode, it helps me adjust."

He nodded in understanding. "Business as usual?"

I grinned. "Yup, exactly."

"Then let's begin. This first time, let me put the headset on you and adjust it for a download. It will feel different, as if something is being pulled out of you. It may take a little getting used to, but then when you get used to it, it can feel almost pleasant."

I nodded. "I remember you thinking that in the mem-unit," I commented. "Do I need to do anything to prepare my mind for a download?"

"Simply put yourself back into that situation. Relive those memories, just as you did when you told them to the League, only this time just witness them…like you're watching an entertainment vid. It will only take a few moments. The system will actually keep you focused on the incidents you wish to download, so don't worry about your mind wandering."

"Interesting," I murmured. "This mem-unit business seems pretty important to the whole PeaceKeeper system."

Bren nodded. "It is. We have found it is the most accurate way to assimilate and transmit truth within our Corps. Nothing is hidden, especially when we can look at the data through all the different frequency levels." He smiled at me. "And are you ready for your first download?"

I swallowed. "I think so."

"Okay, then. Just relax and I'll put the headgear on you like so," he said, adjusting the harness so the receptive nodes touched the centers they were supposed to on my skull.

"Now, Rose, I want you to focus on your first meeting with Sam, and then just allow your thoughts to flow through those events. When you are focused, let me know and I will turn the unit on. Remember, there will be a strange sensation, but no discomfort."

I took a deep breath and put myself back to the day I met Sam. When I had the memory firmly in my thoughts, I nodded to Bren, who touched a panel on the desk and the headset sprang to life. I felt and heard a soft, electrical buzz in my head and then felt an odd pulling sensation that was, as Bren had said, hard to describe.

I forced myself to relax and go with it, closing my eyes and watching all my memories and reactions to those memories flow out of me. It was such an odd experience, reliving all my feelings in fast-forward. Moments later, I was done. The machine seemed to know when the entire experience had been downloaded, because it clicked off and the tugging stopped. The buzzing went silent. I opened my eyes in surprise.

Bren was studying me. "Well?" he asked.

I shook my head. "Another weird experience. Thanks for the heads-up about the strange sensation."

"Do you feel relief?" he wanted to know.

I shook my head. "Not really. Maybe when I get more used to it."

"I asked, because you might like to have your own

personal unit to document your experiences. Only you could access it, and you could make it available to others if you ever wanted to share information."

"I'll think about it," I told him. "I suppose it would be like a diary of sorts. And I could play with the different frequencies, couldn't I?"

He nodded.

"That could help me understand the differences between 3rd, 5ths and 7ths." I murmured. "Say, where are the 4ths and the 6ths?"

"There are no 4ths and 6ths," he answered. "Those are more like frequencies a sentient evolves through. We have different names for those experiences. An Awakening 3rd is one who is evolving into a 5th. A Border 5th is one who is evolving into the frequency of a 7th and so forth." He paused. "I suppose you could call an Awakening 3rd a Fourth and a Border 5th a Sixth, but it would not be entirely accurate. All Keepers and Guardians are operating within frequencies similar to an Awakening 3rd, but it is not our true nature. Our true natures are 5ths. And Watchers mainly consist of 7ths."

"Is Ian a 7th, then?" I asked.

Bren shook his head. "If he were a 7th, he would be unable to create those magnificent algorithms of his. He can science out anything, even things people go to a lot of trouble to keep hidden."

I nodded. "Hence the name Code Breaker, right?"

He nodded and grinned. "It is a gift he does enjoy cultivating."

"So what are you? Are you a 5th?"

Bren smiled and shrugged. "Before my integration with this corpus, I would have called myself a 5th or a Border 5th. I kept myself from evolving so I could remain within the Corps."

"You can do that?"

"It is always about choice. I chose to do this. For the Corps."

I looked at him, wondering if that kind of dedication was ever rewarded. It didn't feel right to me. But then, I was a mere 3rd, so what did I know? "And so what are you since your integration with the corpus?" I asked, adding, "And for that matter, what am I?"

Bren rubbed the back of his neck. "I can tell you what we are not, Rose. I am no longer a 5th and you are no longer an Awakening 3rd. What we are, however, has yet to be defined. I believe we will do that together."

I nodded. "Let's get the party started then, shall we?"

He smiled. "I first need to take my memories of bringing you here from my mem-unit and upload them onto the League's section. Then we can go to my brother's home."

He glanced at me. "Oh, sorry, I didn't mean to assume. Is that plan agreeable?"

I patted his hand. It was the first time I had reached out to him for any other reason than support or comfort, and afterward I wasn't really sure how I felt about it. "It's definitely agreeable. I'm looking forward to the feel of stable, solid ground beneath my feet. And I need some privacy to sort through everything."

"So did I," he said, rising to go to his room to transfer his memories from one mem-unit to another. He turned back at his door. "This won't take long, so I suggest you start packing."

* * *

Bren teleported Ian and me down to Montorea's surface. It was my first teleport, and I felt faint when we arrived at the doorstep of a rather ordinary-looking home, one I could find in any neighborhood back on Earth.

I staggered, and Bren naturally put his arm about me, steadying me. And I must have looked as pale as I felt, because when the door opened revealing a woman and two curious sets of little-boy-eyes peering from behind her, the woman immediately told Ian to distract his sons and Bren to say good-bye to me. With a bemused expression, Bren hugged me good-bye, and reminded me he was available whenever I needed him.

Then I was whisked away, down a fragrant hallway with windows opening to the front street. We entered a pale yellow bedroom, and Domena gently escorted me to a chair in the small sitting area at the end of the bed.

The woman sat across from me, forearms on her thighs, hands clasped. We eyed one another for a few moments in silence. I felt wary, yet curious. This woman was Ian's wife. And Ian was kind.

I knew she was much older, but she appeared to be my own age. And very beautiful, with a mane of thick, golden hair she wore loose and free, swept off her face and falling well below her shoulders. She had a small, pointed chin, a little bow-shaped mouth, straight nose and--I felt my own widening--deep green kitty-cat eyes.

My first alien-looking person.

But those eyes radiated gentle kindness, and, besides, I've always been a cat lover.

I closed my eyes briefly and took a deep breath so I could apologize for my behavior, but she spoke first.

"My dear, you are just a child," she said kindly.

"I may be small, but I am mighty," I replied automatically. I don't remember where I had picked up that slogan, but I used it a lot. It suited me, and it never failed to make me smile.

The woman liked it, too. She threw back her head and laughed—a lovely, clear tone. "I certainly did not mean to offend you," she said, her eyes smiling like a cat's. "I am Domena, Ian's bondmate. Welcome, welcome, my dear. I am so happy and honored you have come here to re-gather yourself."

"Re-gather," I repeated. "That's a good way of putting it." As hard as I tried not to, my voice trembled.

"You poor, darling child," she said. "It must have been a terrible shock for you."

The sincerity in her voice undid me.

I nodded mutely, feeling the tears burn my eyes. When she gathered me to her, I didn't protest. Just clung to her as she stroked my back and murmured gentle, mothering words. I allowed her to undress me down to my underwear and tuck me into the bed, all the time speaking soft, soothing words.

Then she went to the wall, to what looked like a thermostat, and set the dial. The lights dimmed and a gentle breeze flowed over me, scented with sweet, lavender-like scents. I thought I heard music, but it was so faint, I could not be sure.

"I have set the room to Deep Sleep mode," Domena explained. "Sleep for as long as you'd like. It is the best healer. We will have plenty of time to get to know one another when you waken." She brushed a cool palm across my forehead and I drifted off to sleep.

The whispered voices woke me, and I lay there, listening as I tried to remember where I was.

"Is she dead?"

"I don't think so."

"Then why isn't she moving?"

"She just doesn't move much when she sleeps."

A snort. "Not like you. You always kick."

"Do not."

"Do so. Why do you think I got my own bed now?"

"Because you're older now, dumbhead."

"I'm not a dumbhead. I'm telling Mother."

"Shhhh. I think she's awake."

They were silent.

"I don't think so. I think she's dead."

"Dare you to poke her."

"You poke her."

"No. You."

"Why me?"

"Because you're younger and won't get into as much trouble if you make her scream."

"I could make her scream?"

The voice sounded too eager. I decided it was time to wake up.

I had been sleeping on my side, so I rolled onto my back, propping myself up on my elbows. Mindful I was only in my underwear, I made sure the covers stayed fairly high.

Two little boys were peering from the foot of my bed, mouths agape. The smaller one, the one with kitty-cat eyes like his mother's, had his small, chubby finger extended, ready to poke something.

I laughed. "And who have we here?" I said, ducking to stifle a yawn.

"We thought you were dead," said the kitty-cat boy. His solemn little face reminded me of someone.

"How come?" I asked.

"Because you've been asleep for so long."

"Oh? And how long is that?"

"A whole day," said the other boy.

"Really?" I replied, surprised. "That's a long time."

"We only sleep that long if we're sick," he assured me.

I shrugged. "Well, I've been through a lot."

I smiled at the older boy until he smiled back.

"You don't look any different," said the kitty cat.

Bren! He reminded me of a baby-Bren.

"Different than dead? It's cuz I'm not dead," I teased.

They both giggled.

"No," said the older boy, "You don't look any different from us. You see," he explained, "we've never seen a 3rd before. We didn't know what to expect."

"Boys!" Domena exclaimed from the doorway.

They both started.

"Is that any way to treat a guest?"

If I could have bottled "sheepish guilt," I could have manufactured it out of their looks at that moment.

I grinned up at Domena as she flashed a quick wink at me before she put on her Mother Face, a universal look that appeared to be trans-humanoid.

Domena crossed her arms and frowned at her children. "Did we not talk of this earlier?" she asked quietly, reasonably. "Did I not tell you our special guest was here to rest and be quiet, and you were to be respectful of her needs?"

Both boys hung their heads as their faces pinked with embarrassment. The eldest shot me a sidelong glance. The younger's thumb slowly found his mouth.

"We're sorry," the eldest said to me.

"Thorry," the little one mumbled from around his thumb.

"That's better," Domena said. "Now, I do believe you have breakfast waiting for you, and just enough time to eat it before your father takes you to school."

As they shuffled out of the room I called out to them. "Have fun at school. I'm looking forward to meeting you properly when you come back home."

The little one smiled around his thumb.

Domena sighed, her gaze following her two sons as they made their way down the hall before she turned back to me. "I am so sorry, Anna Rose Malone, for my boys' behavior."

I waved a hand. "Please call me Rose. As for your boys, I find them delightful. They're such..." I shrugged, "...typical boys. It's refreshing." I laughed. "The elder was telling the younger to poke me to make sure I wasn't dead."

Domena chuckled, "That's Carlin. He is always convincing Agnar to do things he shouldn't." She moved into the room and opened the drapes. "I can assure you you will have a very quiet morning once they are gone."

She turned, assessing me with those strange eyes, very Sphinx-like. "You look rested. Much better, in fact. How are you feeling?"

I stretched. "Extremely rested, thank you." I glanced at the thermostat-looking device on the wall. "I don't know what you did with all those settings, but I can honestly say I have not slept so well in a very long time."

"Excellent," she said, clasping her hands. "Later, I will show you what this device can do so you can create your own atmosphere."

"Is that what a Harmonist does?" I asked.

She laughed, a delightfully warm sound. "That is just a small part of it, but I will tell you more if you'd like," she said over her shoulder while she went to the closet and withdrew a silky, light blue robe she handed to me.

"I would like that," I replied, nodding my thanks and slipping my arms through the cool fabric. "I love learning new things."

I got out of bed and belted the robe about my waist. It fell gracefully to the floor.

*I **gratefully** acknowledge the following peeps that have supported and helped me with this book—thanks, guys!*

The Beta Readers:

Anni Adrian, Dani Osborn and Michal Mugrage

The Resident Wizard and Editor Extraordinaire:

Faith Freewoman

The Resident Geek:

Julia Freewoman

The Namer of Things:

Cindy Shepard

The Fellow Proofreader:

Greg Shepard

And Last But Not Least:

Those two patient souls who lived through my meltdowns and late meals

Mr. Al and my Sonshine, Cole

ABOUT THE AUTHOR

C.B. Williams (that's me) lives on five acres in the Northern California redwoods with my husband, son, three dogs, four cats and the wild things sharing their space with us.

When I'm not writing or blogging about my adventures, you can find me either painting, playing or adventuring.

For more information about my books, please visit these sites--

Amazon Author Page

Facebook: C. B. Williams

Twitter: @cynthiabryn

Weblog: Chronicles of Cammy

I love to hear from my readers, so feel free to contact me.

Website: www.cbwilliams.us

Email: cb@cbwilliams.us

TO BE PUBLISHED IN THE FALL OF 2014:

ANOTHER SPACE OPERA / LOVE STORY, (WITH ACROBATS!)

OTHER TITLES By C. B. Williams

Under the name Cynthia Campbell Williams:

This Fools Journey, Tarot Tales For Modern Minds (2011)

Under the name C. B. Williams:

The Walkers Trilogy

Walkers (2012)

The Place Between Worlds (2012)

The Shield (2013)